PLAYING

Paul Magrs was born in 1969 on Tyneside. He was brought up in Newton Aycliffe and educated at Woodham Comprehensive, then at Lancaster University, where he took the MA in Creative Writing. He has published a highly acclaimed novel, *Marked For Life*, and his new novel, *Does It Show?* has just been published by Chatto & Windus.

BY PAUL MAGRS

Marked For Life
Does It Show?
Playing Out

Paul Magrs

PLAYING OUT

V

VINTAGE

A VINTAGE BOOK

Published by Vintage 1997

2 4 6 8 10 9 7 5 3 1

First published in Great Britain by
Vintage, 1997

Vintage
Random House, 20 Vauxhall Bridge Road,
London SW1V 2SA

Random House Australia (Pty) Limited
20 Alfred Street, Milsons Point, Sydney
New South Wales 2061, Australia

Random House New Zealand Limited
18 Poland Road, Glenfield,
Auckland 10, New Zealand

Random House South Africa (Pty) Limited
Endulini, 5A, Jubilee Road, Parktown 2193,
South Africa

Random House UK Limited Reg. No. 954009

A CIP catalogue record for this book
is available from the British Library

ISBN 0 09 973571 7

Papers used by Random House UK Ltd are natural,
recyclable products made from wood grown in sustain-
able forests. The manufacturing processes conform to
the environmental regulations of the country of origin

Typeset in 10½/12 Sabon by
Palimpsest Book Production Limited,
Polmont, Stirlingshire
Printed and bound in Great Britain by
Cox & Wyman, Reading, Berkshire

A VINTAGE ORIGINAL

Contents

Patient Iris   1
Ariel's Tasty Dog   6
Seven Disenchantments   19
Judith's Do Round Hers   27
The Furrier the Better   52
Emma's Situation   64
Laminating Ideal Men   76
Anemones, My Labrador, His Puppy   91
The Lion Vanishes   107
Ocarina   118
The Giant Spider's Supervisor   127
Those Imaginary Cows   140
Bargains for Charlotte   155
Cold Companionable Streams   164
Will You Stay in Our Lovers' Story?   172
Could It Be Magic?   179

This book is for my brother, Mark Magrs

With thanks to . . .
(in order of appearance)

Joy Foster, Charles Foster, Louise Foster, Lynne Heritage, Nicola Cregan, Katherine Williamson, Jane Woodfine, Pete Courtie, Brigid Robinson, Suzi Stephens, Paul Arvidson, Andrea Greenwood, Julia Wiggston, Laura Wood, Steve Jackson, Gene Hult, Jon Rolfe, Antonia Rolfe, Richard Wilson, Lynne Pearce, Alicia Stubbersfield, Siri Hansen, Joan Diamond, Kelly Gerrard, Paul Cornell, David Craig, Gabrielle Rowe, Colin Swallow, Leigh Pain, Bill Penson, Alan Bennett, Mark Walton, Daryl Spears, Sara Maitland, Meg Davis, Amanda Reynolds, Richard Klein, A. S. Byatt, Jonathan Burnham, Claire Patterson, Sara Holloway and everyone at Chatto.

'Patient Iris' was first published in *New Writing 4*, 'Anemones, My Labrador, His Puppy' in *New Writing 5*, and 'Emma's Situation' in the 1995 Darius anthology, *Watchfire*.

PATIENT IRIS

SHE HAS A friend called Patient Iris who lives at the top of the town by the Roman remains.

Irises take a good while to open. She thinks if you place them by the window they stand a better chance.

Iris is patient. She watches men reconstructing the Roman remains.

At the top of the town you can see all of South Shields, the grey flank of North Shields, the blue sash of sea.

The Romans must have built here for the view.

Their fort is vast. When they rebuild it, do they use the old stones or do they have all new, cut into shapes they have guessed at? She and Patient Iris watch them working and the stone certainly looks new. Newer and more yellow than even those private estates they've been putting up.

She feels bad about Patient Iris. Who has turned bright yellow and sits by the phone. Who is ready to ring out in case she has an emergency. Her bedsores are a sight to see. She has looked under Patient Iris's nightgown, at Patient Iris's bidding. She instructed Patient Iris to sit by her window, to get some air, watch the world outside. Lying down all day does you no good in the end.

Fat purple welts, all down the back of her. Succulent, like burst fruit.

Patient Iris can't quite remember, but didn't the coast here once freeze entirely?

It is so high up. The Roman soldiers, with the north wind

shushing up their leather skirts, parading on those ramparts, must have had it hard.

And didn't it once freeze over?

Patient Iris lived at the end of a street. When the coast froze up, surely it was before the time they bombed the row's other end? The houses went down like dominoes, a trail of gunpowder, stopping just short of Iris's door.

Patient Iris is a survivor. She survived the freezing-over that winter when, she realises now, she must still have been a child.

She talks on the phone with her friend. Her friend phones now more often than she visits. They both agree that visiting is not much use. There's nothing new to see. Although the Roman remains, across the way, grow a little higher every day.

And these two women don't need to see each other. They are so accustomed to the sight that the phone is all they need. And it saves Iris's friend a trip out. Up the hill is arduous work, after all. Yet they used to walk it happily, to get to the Spiritualist church. When calling up your husband was the thing, before bingo.

Her friend phones to check up on Patient Iris's back. Both know that her health can't last this winter.

And winter is stealing in. When Patient Iris wakes in her chair each morning, the first thing she sees is the Roman remains blanched white with scabs of frost, their outlines etched in by an impossibly blue sky.

Winters like this, everything turns to jewels. Patient Iris runs her fingers over and round her tender sores as she speaks into the receiver to her oldest living friend. Will they turn to rubies, drop away, make her well again and rich?

'Do you remember –' she says, breaking into her friend's flow. 'Do you remember when the coast froze up?'

Her friend is thrown for a moment. Then she sees the orange cranes frozen in the docks, useless and wading on ice. The monstrous keels of half-completed ships, abandoned, like wedding dresses on dummies with the arms not on yet and pins sticking out.

2

'I think so,' she mumbles. She had been telling Patient Iris about the local women, bonded in a syndicate, who won a million pounds between them on the football pools. They were all supermarket cashiers and had their photos taken by the local press, sitting in shopping trolleys.

'But do you remember the seals on the ice?' They appeared from nowhere. Came thousands of miles south because it was so cold that winter.

Her friend doesn't remember the seals.

Patient Iris recalls seeing grey sides of beef stranded on ice. She worked in a butchers, running errands. The butcher boys joked about serving up seal chops.

The seals grew bigger. From the top of the town Patient Iris could hear them bark at night. Not like dogs; grunting coughs like old men in the park. They were getting bigger because they were pregnant. The whiskered seals with large, inscrutable eyes, beached on the useless docks.

'Imagine,' says Patient Iris suddenly. 'Imagine giving birth on sheer ice. Imagine being born on sheer ice. You come out of blubbery safety, straight into snow. The seals try to cover each other, but . . .'

Her friend decides Iris's mind is wandering. Tomorrow she will visit her in person. She begins to end the phone call. She wants Iris to put down the phone in case she needs to phone herself an ambulance. She knows Patient Iris all too well and how she likes to do things for herself.

Patient Iris has been kneading the bedsores as she talks. Down the side of her leg, through stiff white cotton, fresh stains of primrose and carmine bloom.

Patient Iris puts down the phone and thinks.

One night when the seals were barking out their birth pangs, she left the house in her nightie and slippers and walked down to the docks.

The dark, slumped shapes, dividing and reproducing, unabashed on the exposed span of gleaming ice. The high pig squeals of baby seals. The mothers rolling over, moist

3

with their own cooling gels, careful not to slip and crush their children.

Patient Iris met a woman, a hag, really, with great hooped skirts and a basket of herring on her back. She said her name was Dolly. She was a lunatic, screaming the odds at the clock face when it struck the hour. In her basket the fish slipped and goggled their frozen eyes as Dolly jogged about to keep warm.

'I keep sailors inside my skirts. That's why I wear them so big. So they can hide inside and dodge the draft. They needn't have to go to sea. Or do what they don't want.'

Dolly's face was like a coconut, the hairs growing thick inside the grooves so she'd never be able to shave them if she tried.

Tonight Iris's oldest living friend dreams of Iris turning yellow and sitting by the phone. The moonlight shines off stark Roman walls and drops into her room.

Patient Iris is still, asleep sitting up, looking dead already. Apart from the slight hiss of breath, which issues as smoke from her open mouth. She is awkward in her chair, doubled up with her precious jumble of ruined organs preserved in that clatter of limbs. She looks just as uncomfortable as those cashiers posing in their shopping trolleys, arms and legs akimbo and waving their champagne glasses and oversized cheques as photographers' bulbs go off.

Patient Iris's friend of many years dreams that this winter will be cold. Colder even than that winter before the town was bombed and Tyne Dock was sheeted over in ice.

Colder still and the men decide to down tools and abandon the Roman remains till spring. It is so cold that it frightens them. This kind of weather will crystallise fragments of lost souls in the air. They rekindle themselves and brighten jewellike when it comes in dark. Centurions gather on the ramparts in their leather skirts with the wind whistling through them, their eyes dead quartz.

In the cold imagined by Iris's friend, the Roman remains can complete themselves.

Old outlines glisten silver on the air, tugging at each other like a big top going up. They stir the air to recall what once stood there. Moisture freezes, clicks into place and recreates a fabulous ice palace on the reconstructed site at the top of the town above the docks.

Patient Iris's window is open and the time is right for irises to open. Unseasonably, perhaps, even dangerously, in midwinter. But what does Patient Iris care for danger now?

She is open to the elements. Her sores expose her to the harshest that the north can offer.

The cold of the north heals up Patient Iris for ever. Her gasping, fishlike internal organs stop collapsing and freeze. Her bedsores harden. Iris reaches with one arthritic hand to splash a little scent behind each ear before she allows the cold to come over her entirely.

Scent catches at each earlobe and dangles there, perfect crystal earrings. And now Patient Iris is sealed for ever. The fate of those at extremes, like here, at the top of the hill.

She decides to pop out for a walk. It is the first time she has fancied walking in ages. Perhaps Dolly is still out there somewhere, saving sailors, or Roman centurions, under her voluminous skirts.

Patient Iris stops by the docks to see the seal mothers return and, sure enough, she is rewarded by the sight of their stolid hard-working, bodies.

She is much braver now that her phone is left off the hook and she can wear her bedsores as jewellery. She will skate over the ice to see how the burgeoning families are doing. She will talk the snorting, whiskered mothers through a difficult night, as their children are slapped out like old shoes onto the bloodied glass.

ARIEL'S TASTY DOG

THAT AFTERNOON HE had a bit of a walk down town with Simon and Kerry. He didn't get down the precinct much. Turned out it hadn't changed since they used to hang about there, Saturday afternoons. Today they walked down with the pushchair and a shopping list. He didn't have anything better waiting.

'I bet there's a lot of shopping you have to get,' he said, 'with a baby, ey? I bet there's loads that the likes of me wouldn't even think of.'

Kerry looked at him. They were halfway up Swaledale Avenue. The nunnery had been knocked down and there was a little street of private houses there now. Simon remarked on it. Both he and Ray remembered jumping the wall of the nunnery on the way home from school, and not getting chased.

'She costs a fortune,' Kerry said and bent to straighten the bairn's sunhat. Ray was laughing at the bairn's efforts to yank it off.

'You know that at the outset, though, don't you? When you have them.' Ray nodded to himself. 'When you have kids . . .' He tailed off because he'd been about to add, 'A kid is for life,' before remembering that was the RSPCA slogan for looking after dogs. He wouldn't make himself popular saying stuff like that.

The town clock bonged out the hour and from the industrial estate came the air-raid wailing for coffeetime in the factories.

'I want to go to Boyes,' Kerry said as they crossed to the

6

arcade. The bairn's wheels stuck on the tall kerb and Simon had to help.

'What does she need now?'

'Not for her,' Kerry snapped. Boyes did cheap kids' clothes – there were real bargains sometimes – and she resented him saying she bought too many things there. She liked keeping the bairn nice. She was a little girl. Simon shouldn't complain. He should keep that complaining tone out of his voice. They were doing all right. 'I want to go there for something else.'

'Right.'

Ray had been quiet since they'd cut through the street where he'd lived when he was about ten. He'd had a birthday party in one of those gloomy houses. Simon had been there, but Kerry hadn't because even though she'd been in the same class she was never really a friend of either of them at that stage.

He remembered Simon staying indoors during the party, while the others ran around, out in the back garden. Ray had been embarrassed because, with everyone just running about in the garden, it wasn't really like a party at all. It was just playing out. He went in and saw that Simon had put his *Jungle Book* record on the stereo. It was old and Ray had meant to hide all that kid stuff.

Simon sat looking at the pictures on the record's sleeve, on the settee next to Ray's mam. She looked shattered, still wearing her rubber gloves from washing up after the birthday tea.

'This picture of Baloo the Bear,' Simon was saying to her. 'See the way he's standing? At home I have a Roto-Draw set that lets you draw him standing in exactly the same . . .' He struggled to find the word. 'In exactly the same *action*.'

Ray's heart went out to him without his really knowing why. Three years later – when they were thirteen – in the school changing rooms after a rugby game, something struck Ray out of the blue. On the bench beside him Simon sat with elbows on knees, shirtless, picking clods of mud out from between the studs on his boots. Ray said, '*Position*. That was the word you wanted. Baloo the Bear in exactly the same *position*.'

7

Simon looked at him in open-mouthed irritation. 'You what?'

In the precinct, under the big ramp, there was a corner made by the front of Boyes and the side of Weigh Your Own. It was all health food and cheap stuff in there, sold loose from drums with see-through lids. Everything was labelled with stencilled lettering because, in the drums, most things looked alike. Stencilled posters covered the windows, telling you how much everything cost per pound.

'SUGAR' 35p lb
Ariel 69p lb
'Radion' 75p lb
Pasta 'Twirls' 29p lb
Omega 'Tasty' dog 72p lb
'Ginger' cake mix 33p lb
Herbs 'n' Spices 'Inside'

They paused in that corner because part of Kerry's usual trip down town was buying a quarter of Flying Saucers sweets from Weigh Your Own and sharing them with the bairn, sitting on a bench. They had a few plants out there now and it was quite a gathering place. Everyone talks to you when you have a bonny bairn with you. Many was the half-hour Kerry had spent talking to someone because they wanted to give the bairn ten pence or tickle her under the chin. Pensioners, usually, who liked to sit on the benches in that corner of the precinct.

Ray and Simon couldn't find space to sit so they just stood about. A crowd had gathered around some buskers. One had a large roll of paper taped to the flagstones. He was drawing with pastel crayons, a purple sunset and a woman clinging to the back of a unicorn, which was flying. His little basket had quite a few coins in.

'Let's nick his fucking basket,' Simon said.

'Ay,' laughed Ray.

Amazingly the busker who was drawing still managed to

sing. He drew left-handed, on his knees, and in his right hand he had his microphone, which was plugged into the same amplifier as his friend's mike and guitar. The song they were doing was 'Unchained Melody' from that video with the feller from *Dirty Dancing* in, *Ghost*. They were doing quite a good job of it.

'They're bloody flat, aren't they?' said Ray.

'Fucking awful. Look at this lot, standing round gawping.' Simon twirled round on his heel. He saw that Kerry was talking to some old woman. The bairn was out of the chair and being passed from knee to knee. That meant they were hanging about for a while. He read the posters on the windows of Weigh Your Own again and scowled.

'Our lass tried to get us onto that soya mince stuff from there.'

'Did she?'

'Like vegetarian soya.'

'Ay, I've seen it on daytime telly, like. What's it taste like?'

'Tastes like nowt. She put three Oxo cubes in with it an' all and it tasted nowt like mince. Bloody rubbish!'

'Ay, well, they'd sell you owt, wouldn't they?'

When 'Unchained Melody' finished everyone clapped. The buskers started 'The Sun Ain't Gonna Shine Anymore'. The one with the guitar was a good bit older than the artist. It was as if he was bringing him on. Or as if the younger one was an apprentice and he was learning a trade. But he was so enthusiastic he was learning to do two things at once.

Simon never knew why she bothered talking to the old bitches. They came out with a load of shite. And the old blokes! Eyeing her up.

'This is the important thing. Education.' The woman was nodding and jogging the bairn on her knee. God, she can't have had more than ten hairs on her head. 'And it's good for you to have something to occupy you, too, isn't it?'

'Oh, yes,' Kerry said.

'I remember. Having bairns and being in all day. You need something. I never had the brains.'

'What's she on about?' Ray asked Simon. 'Scruffy old bitch!'

'Ay, Kerry's let her have our bairn on her knee, an' all! Ah, she's telling her all about that course of hers.'

'What for?' Without realising it, Ray was tapping his foot to the buskers' playing.

'And it's an English course, you say?'

Kerry nodded.

'I've got a grandbairn gonna do her GCSE English this year. She's very good at English. Spell anything you like. I can't put two words together so it can't be my side of the family she gets it from.'

'I want to go on and do it at university.'

'Well, I wish you luck, pet. There should be more women going off to places like that. College educations. They reckon it's happening, though, don't they?'

'I'll do it from home. Part time, like.'

'That's good. English. It's like I told Lisa – that's my grandbairn, the eldest one – when she was choosing which exams to take in her GCSEs. I said, your maths and your English are the most important ones, pet. That's what they always ask for. Your writing and your numbers. That's what you're gonna need. The teacher agreed with me, like. Lisa took my advice. Will you be doing maths?'

Kerry smiled and reached over to take the bairn, who was getting bored now, sucking on a pulped handful of Flying Saucers. 'Just the English,' she said. 'It's enough for me.'

Buckling the bairn into her chair, she added, without knowing why, 'I'm reading *The Tempest* at the moment. For my course.'

'Are you?' The woman was tapping her feet to the buskers now and she looked vague, as if she'd forgotten what they'd been on about.

'By Shakespeare.'

'Shakespeare, eh? Well, then.'

'It's about a fairy called Ariel.' Kerry looked about, getting ready to go into Boyes. 'Well, I've only read the first scene or so.'

'My attention goes,' said the woman and with her fingers combed her hair which had flapped loose in the breeze. 'I read a few lines of something and honestly, if you were to ask me what it was about, I'd not have the first idea. It's just me, man. I'm daft.'

Kerry stood with the pushchair in the hardware aisle and as she stared at the display of little packets of tacks and nails she had tears bursting up in her eyes. Boyes was empty and musicless and so she could hear her husband and Ray, over in the cheap records and ornaments, laughing.

'It's about a fairy called Ariel. She bloody lives in books.' That laughing in Ray's voice she remembered from school, his accent thicker than ever in mockery.

'Fucking Ariel the fairy!' She could almost hear Simon shaking his head. It was as if the bairn were listening in too, she was so still and quiet.

Kerry hardly knew what she was looking at. Screws and pins and needles and that. All different sizes, lengths, types. A short man with a dark tache and a striped shirt came over to her, his nylon trousers whishing up the aisle. His badge said 'Derek'. 'Can I help?'

Simon was shaking his head ruefully, his voice taunting. 'Ariel the fucking fairy!'

'Sixty-nine pee a pound!' Ray laughed. 'Ariel the fucking fairy – 69p a pound!' They both laughed.

'Washes fucking whiter an' all!' Simon said, too loud.

Derek kept his eyes on Kerry and waited for her reply, determined not to hear the laughter a few aisles away.

Kerry said, 'I want to put up a whole wallful of shelves as cheaply as possible.'

'Listen, listen, man . . .' Ray was giggling like a kid, almost painfully, as if he was about to wet himself. They were both in a silly mood, poking through Boyes' cheap goods. Simon held up two flower-fairy fridge magnets.

'Look at this fucking rubbish!'

Ray laughed a laugh like a snort either side of his mouth. Simon made the fridge magnets do a dance.

'Listen, man,' Ray said, still laughing.

'Paul bloody Newman's salad dressing! Looks like his spunk in a bloody bottle.'

'Ugh, shurrup, man! Listen – Ariel's tasty dog!'

There was a pause. 'What?'

They both remembered, at school, when someone would come out with a new word or phrase that would take off. They could become brilliant insults if used right and had to be coined with love. Ray had excelled at buzz words. He laid claim to classics: 'foy dog', 'fester cat', 'dipshit', all had been his once upon a time. He'd hear people all over school, saying his words, laughing. Neither he nor Simon had heard a good one in years. But this had the feel of something good.

'Say it again,' said Simon, starting to giggle.

'Ariel's "tasty" dog. Like on the poster in Weigh Your fuckin' Own.'

'Ariel's tasty "dog".'

'"Ariel's" tasty dog.'

'Ariel's "tasty" dog.'

They laughed again.

Blushing, Kerry listened to Derek telling her how chipboard was her best bet, but she'd have to buy it down Homeplan and cover it with something. Sticky-backed plastic. Thirty-eight pence a square foot it used to be ... He rushed for his calculator and slid it out of its smart plastic wallet. 'I've not done these kinds of sums in ages. Hope I can still do them. Now, what lengths do you want?'

'Ariel's tasty dog.'

'The wall's about twelve feet long. And I want shelves down to the floor ... from the ceiling. About five ... shelves down.'

'Have you got a lot of plants and ornaments then, pet?'

'Books. I've got a lot of books everywhere round the house. Thousands of them in boxes. Cluttering up. I want them putting right.'

'Thing is, the chipboard only comes in eight-foot lengths.'

'Oh.'

' "Ariel's" tasty dog.'

'So I reckon . . . do three sets of five, four foot long each.'

'What? Oh . . . yeah.'

'But don't do them right across, like one long shelf. To make it good, like, um . . .'

'Stagger them?'

'Do one set, then set the next set, like, halfway down a bit . . . so they're, like, staggered. Then you've got . . . ends at either side. Like bookends. And that'll look really smart.'

'Ariel's "tasty" dog.'

'When you said stick them up with grey brackets . . . ?'

'You get them here.' He went and picked up a handful of the grey L's. 'Twenty pence each.'

'That's cheap.'

'There's nowt to them. You drill in these, put the plug in the wall and that expands so they don't come out again and you screw in your screw. Oh. Is your wall brick or, like, cavitied?'

Kerry pictured it. Last winter when the pipes went funny something discharged itself endlessly, night and day, inside that wall. It had definitely sounded like a cavity. Christmas she had spent reading in the kitchen listening to the cavity filling up with water. She told Derek this. He frowned.

'That doesn't sound very good, does it?' He fished out a packet of plugs. 'Anyway, these are for, like, cavitied plasterboard walls.'

'Oh . . . it's an outer wall I'm on about.'

'Then that's what you call a brick wall. You want the other plugs.'

'Right.' Kerry straightened up. She glanced across and the bairn was looking restless, a packet of curtain hooks wedged into her mouth. 'I'll not get stuff now. I've got to go home and find out whether we've got a drill or not.'

'This is the bit you want. A twelve or an eight.'

'Oh. Right.'

'Your own place, is it?'

13

'Ariel's tasty "fucking" dog!'

Derek shook his head. 'I'm sorry about them lads.'

She took off the bairn's brake. 'Yeh. It's me own place.'

'Well, I hope you get your shelves sorted out.'

'I'll be back.'

'Aw, look, man, you'll love this. Look!'

Kerry came back into the front room to see Simon, his voice raised excitedly, dragging out his Picnic Cool Box.

'You'll fucking love this.'

'What is it?' Here Ray was less sure of himself. He was much less cocky in Kerry's house. Simon had set the white plastic chest between two armchairs in front of the telly. He flipped open the lid to show Ray it was full of cans of lager, all kept cool. 'Look – we leave it right here. It's all ready for the fuckin' World Cup.'

'Ariel's tasty dog!' Ray said and sat down in the chair next to Simon. They opened a can of lager each.

'The bairn's just gone off to sleep,' Kerry said, heading for the kitchen. 'Keep your voice down a bit.'

They didn't say anything but when she was in the kitchen she could hear through the serving hatch that Simon said 'Ariel's tasty dog' again.

The kitchen table was stacked with the paperbacks she was reading just now – *The Go-Between*, *The Tempest*, *Emma* and York Notes on all three of them. Her A4 pad was out and a reporter's book of pencilled notes. The kitchen noticeboard was a collage of the bairn's scribbles and potato prints and Kerry's clippings and marked essays and forms. On the cooker pans were bubbling and she had about twenty-five minutes to read before dinner needed to go out.

Scene One was a long one in *The Tempest*. She liked the name Miranda and wished she'd thought of it before, to give to the bairn. They'd settled on Julie.

When she had shelves up, covering the length and height of the outer wall of their bedroom, would she arrange her books alphabetically? Or would she put them in any old order, for the fun of seeing what ended up rubbing shoulders with what?

*   *   *

14

The football was finished and they had made a little pyramid of their empty cans on top of the telly. They were throwing the bairn's toys to knock them off.

'Tea's ready,' Kerry said. 'Are you stopping for your tea, Ray?'

Ray held up a spongy dog with floppy ears. It was Julie's first toy. Simon had brought it to the hospital. 'Ariel's tasty dog!' Ray cackled. He sniffed the toy and smacked his lips. 'Ariel's "tasty" dog!' With that he bit off one of the spongy dog's ears.

'Ha ha ha ha ha!' He spat it out and threw the toy down. Then he saw that Simon wasn't laughing.

'The bairn's had that since she was born, you tit!'

'So?'

'So you've fuckin' knacked it. I bought that for her when she was born!'

'Oh.'

Kerry picked the dog up. She asked Simon, 'Have we got a drill?'

Ray looked worried. 'What?'

'I want to put my own shelves up. Like staggered shelves up. For my books.'

'I've got a drill somewhere. What are we going to do with the bairn's dog?'

'Well,' she said. 'It's bloody ruined, isn't it? Your mate's bloody ruined it.'

Ray tried to make them laugh. 'But it was Ariel's tasty dog!'

Kerry tossed the dog into Simon's Picnic Cool Box. 'Get out of my house, Ray. Don't fucking come back.'

They were in bed early that night. Kerry tended to stay awake later, sitting up to read. She was still on with her Shakespeare. Simon was getting so that he hated the cover of that book. It was an old-fashioned one, and reminded him of the books in school.

'Ariel's tasty dog,' he murmured to himself, lying away from her as she read.

'What?' she asked, and the phone rang.

They let it go a few times, down in the hall.

'It's past midnight,' she breathed.

'Something's happened,' he said, sitting up now.

'It'll be your mam. She's died.'

'It could be anyone. Anyone could have . . . had an accident.'

The rings went on.

'Aw, get it,' Kerry said. 'It'll have the bairn awake.'

He got up and went downstairs in his underpants. They were partly rucked up and she saw he had a spot coming on his bum. Funny, she thought, what you notice. The ringing stopped and she listened hard to catch what Simon was saying. She couldn't pick it out so she looked at the book again, but nothing would stick. She realised her heart was hammering away. It was as Simon had said, when he was drunk and sentimental on New Year's Eve, having a bairn made you scared of many more things. And that included the phone ringing when you weren't expecting it. It was as if your nerves were made to stretch further. She was pleased Simon felt like that too.

He came back. 'I don't believe him.'

'Who?' She pushed *The Tempest* away as Simon slid back under the quilt, shivering.

'Bloody Ray! He's out in Darlington. Pissed out of his head. Ringing up, all upset. He wanted to apologise, he said.'

'He what? Ray?'

'He wanted to talk to you, really, but I told him you were asleep. He's bloody crackers. He reckons that, tomorrow, he's gonna go round all the shops in Darlington to look for a toy dog exactly like the one he ruined.'

Simon snuggled down to sleep again. She listened to his five-o'clock shadow scrape on the pillow. She had a very hairy husband. Hirsute, she corrected herself.

'He phoned after midnight to say that?'

Simon looked round. 'He also said we were his favourite friends.'

She tutted. 'Favourite bloody friends!'

16

'He's a nutcase.'

'He's your bloody friend, not mine.'

Simon's hand slid across to her under the quilt. She watched its impression beneath the fabric, thinking of *Jaws*. He said, 'He's just Ariel's tasty dog.'

'Don't start that again!'

In the next room the bairn started wailing.

'Shite!'

'I'll go,' Kerry said, though it wasn't her turn. She was better at quieting her.

Simon groaned. 'It's like having two kids.'

When Kerry went to see her she was standing up in the cot, clinging to the bars and rocking backwards and forwards, yelling her head off. She's a gutsy one, Kerry thought. She's gonna have a right life, this one. She picked her up and she wasn't wet or anything. She was just cross.

Mother and daughter had taken to having midnight traipses around the back garden. The bairn had come to expect them. She was just reminding her mam. As soon as Kerry took her down the stairs, into the kitchen, the bairn shut up. She gurgled, even, as Kerry opened the back door and stepped out into the gravid summer air. The lawn and bushes of dock leaves and nettles, all their hedges, were a deep mysterious blue. Kerry's bare feet shushed through the grass.

'You know, I wish we *had* called you Miranda,' she told her daughter.

Julie just cooed with her head facing backwards over Kerry's shoulder, as if she was being winded. She cooed because something had caught her eye.

Kerry turned, to squint at the bottom of the garden, trying to see what the bairn's keen and milky-blue eyes had seen.

A lithe, bone-white, quite hairless fairy eased himself from under the hedge. He didn't notice Kerry as she held her breath and gripped the bairn tighter. Ariel was intent on his mustard-coloured pit-bull terrier, which had shot under the hedgerow ahead of him and was now digging a hole in the lawn.

Simon will go crackers about his lawn, Kerry was thinking. He was painstaking when he laid that. It was like carpeting. And that was what he had been meant to be looking out for in Boyes this afternoon – shears – but Ray had kept distracting him.

Soon the dog had made a sizeable hole and moonlight glinted off something down there. Kerry assumed it was a bone but the grunting yellow dog took it out and laid it carefully on the grass. Then Ariel gave him a swift pat and they both bolted back into the undergrowth.

She watched a moment and then went to see. They had left her a spanking new drill, minus its bit. Julie clapped her hands. Well, Kerry thought, we can buy the right-size bit from Boyes, from Derek.

SEVEN DISENCHANTMENTS

UNTIL THE VERY end my grandfather kept a suitcase with him. 'I'll fight it tooth and nail, every step of the frigging way, and they'll never get hold of it.'

The last time I saw him, in the home, where he died exhaling the dust of his carefully cluttered *objets*, he was clutching the case to his chest, struggling with inarticulate hands at the clasps.

His stockinged feet, meanwhile, curled about the gramophone which sat like a faithful hound. He was basking in crackling, booming Puccini arias. 'I've taken up opera – me! Frigging opera!' His feet, far steadier than hands, stroked the wooden gramophone's sides. 'I've found it's the best there is for vibration. The vibration warms up my feet. When you start to die, it's the frigging feet as gets hit first.'

How long would his shaken form hold up? I wondered. Opera couldn't keep him warm indefinitely. I stepped past the bric-a-brac and the pleasantries, asking, 'You wanted me for something?'

When he looked up there was fear and defiance in those eyes, a blue translucence like the finest china, cracked and patched with threads of dirty yellow glue. He must have decided I was an accomplice. Relenting, he said, 'This suitcase. It has to be kept away from them.'

'What's inside it?'

'Your frigging inheritance, my lad.'

'Shall I open it now?'

I have always enjoyed opening presents. Despite what they say, the pleasure is neither in giving nor receiving.

19

It is always in opening, for giver and receiver both. The *jouissance* of discovery, the shattering of bondage. As a child I anticipated a career in either burglary or escapology. Penetration and extrication have always been my areas of expertise. I could never stand a cluttered room or a bolted entrance. It strikes me now that, even during the gaudiest of sexual permutations enacted by my person, I have submitted to very few enacted upon – or within – my person. I have always been the Alcatraz of sexual partners – immune and integral, even at the point of crisis.

In this particular scene, I must admit, my grandfather's suitcase had me more than intrigued. I could not help it; an erotic frisson charges the air of any present-giving I am party to, whether that gift is a person, a unique opportunity or a device of some kind, which only I can open.

'I've kept it till the bloody end, unopened – for you, son. Only you can open it. It's all yours.'

I wrenched it from his feeble grasp, kicking the gramophone and causing the needle to shriek across several grooves as I did so. The music startled and hissed; a delicious death rattle halfway through 'O mio babbino caro'. With that, I thought I myself might die from pleasure, the scene was so rich, piquant with resonances. The old man settled back under the music's upswing, toes curling at the edge of the box, the oily sheen of the record's surface reflecting dully in his bifocals, and I set to attacking the rusted hinges, buckles and clasps of his precious suitcase.

'Because you're frigging choosy, aren't you? Just like your old grandad. Well, here's something to see you right. Make proper use of it and you'll never be wanting!'

I'll never be wanting. I have wanted for nothing. You were wrong, grandad; frigging wrong. I have wanted. I have wanted badly. You could never see me right. You never even saw me open the suitcase, saw me react. Just as well, perhaps, as at first, I was wholly underwhelmed at the gift. Monumentally pissed off, as it happens, with what I had to smuggle out of your room, out of the rest home, while

20

matron checked you over, slipped shut your eyelids, called the coroner and so on.

You never wrote your will down, you old bastard. So I had to thieve the thing, effectively, in order to carry out your wishes. And your wishes involved my being bequeathed . . . this. Well, well.

Like any good giver of presents you understood the psychology involved. The receiver is to be seduced. They want to have their wishes taken away from them, their power of choice and responsibility frazzled away in the acid bath of somebody else's hierarchy of value. I, like everyone else, wanted to be whisked away, swirled into the updraught of the desires you had projected upon the space allotted to my own . . . and set down again in a new set of circumstances defined by your gift.

You gave me that, and I thank you. But in the past I have cursed you. This is a moral little tale, I suppose, by virtue of the fact that I have indeed come to a bad end. I can't help that; many do. I probably shan't *sound* moral.

You see, I was given a lack of choice. My desires were plucked out of the air for me. They solidified and took on life, based on woolly presumptions of what I might like.

And I . . . I wasted them. I stretched my desires hard; they snapped back like rubber bands.

I once knew a man who collected rubber bands, dropped by the postman or schoolgirls in the roadside. He said you never knew when they might 'come in'. I said they might have been anywhere. I buy new rubber bands when I need them. And I waste them shamelessly. In fact, I'm the one who drops them by the roadside. All mine are snapped, like old knicker elastic; they will never 'come in' for anything.

I am voracious and fickle. That was my downfall. If I point to a moral by having a downfall; so be it. I also had a rise and a rise and a rise . . . pointing to a different moral, I hope. Voracious and fickle; you stretch as far as you may go and push on and push on and scratch and claw, bellow and rant your way on and out and into sheer, certain disaster and the cliff edge of workaday morality skids from under your soles and then . . . you are propelled back to your original state. Where you may bleat of morality, warn others of stretching their elasticised bondage. Or you relish the telling as you soar ever onwards, Oz-bound on the cyclone of your desires, the knicker elastic snapped and shrivelled like a severed umbilical cord behind you.

Fickle as ever; I like to think of myself like that. That is; immoral and with my knicker elastic around my ankles.

It's spot-the-contradiction time.

Having stressed my absolute nonpassivity, I go on to chat about the bliss of having one's desires imposed – almost brutally – upon one's person. It's a slippery slope, passivity; one I've been down many a time.

And inside the suitcase, you ask?

A book with empty pages. When I took it home I thought. Screw this particular symbolic frisson for a lark! Grandfather had handed me my future, to inscribe it for myself. The world was an empty page at my fingertips. No, this isn't a story about writing. God forbid. I never wrote. This isn't a story, it hasn't a moral. For tucked in between the pages were seven pressed flowers. I counted them. They were different sorts. I know nothing about flowers so I can't describe them. Some were prettier than others.

My grandfather's message, on the flyleaf: 'Drop them in water and watch them come to life . . . only one at a time . . . when you've had enough of one, try the next.'

Japanese paper flowers. They expand in a delicate china bowl, swim out through the centre of the water, reel and span their allotted globe . . . I decided to try one out.

My first flower was the man with the elastic bands. He wasted nothing; we traipsed the streets together looking for odds and ends. We hunted through junk shops and he, like Grandfather, cluttered out the place he occupied, rent-free. It was a barge on a canal. When we made love, below the water level, we could hear the keel slap and rumble on the external pressure. There was a glass floor and one night, glancing sideways, I saw two badgers swimming below our boat. One bared his fangs and scratched the glass. My lover threw a rug over them, to keep them out.

He was, I suppose, a kind of ideal man, though he never struck me as that at the time. Michelangelo's David? Masculinity that can afford to be fey, slouched at the steering deck, hand on hip as we foraged down the ship canal, me bent out of sight, sucking him off as he called out to fellow sailors that passed us by. His prick reminded me of a prawn; there was something fishy about him altogether, I decided. Eventually I threw him back, and tried another flower.

A big box of chocolates which, in my mood, didn't last long at all. My canal-faring days were over; my lover, quite naturally, had vanished the same moment that the chocolates appeared. Nothing unnatural about that. How many men sail off into the night and leave behind a confectionery surrogate?

And all because the gentleman loves a good surrogate . . . I gobbled them up quicker than I had the prawn, hidden on my knees on his poop deck.

Then came the lady with the fruit. She stepped straight out of the Pre-Raphaelite catalogue. I was secretly ashamed at whatever unconscious desires I had, through her apparition, articulated. I felt I was somehow denigrating women with this stereotypical flame-haired beauty, recumbent on the sort of marble flooring rendered exquisitely by Alma-Tadema. We had pomegranates everywhere, crushing and popping their juicy cells like fragrant frogspawn in the clash and lick of thighs and hips.

A thigh and hip diet full of vitamin C . . . then the meatier, more equatorial juices, the colonial issues that I admit I probed for as if they were indeed an elixir of life. Does this denigrate her? Did my idyll of Michelangelo denigrate my prawn-pricked lover on the canal? What denigrated them most, perhaps, was the utter dejuicing enacted upon them. I have, in my time, extracted juices. I am the man from Del Monte, declaring the eternal 'Yes!' in my white hat and resilient, immaculate suit. It is stained when seen up close. I left them both as husks; the pulped rinds and kernels scattered in my wake.

A cellar full of wine. I was thirty by now and dying for a drink. I got pissed for a while. That was a poppy, that flower. I know that one; the fumes were intoxicating even before its heady incarnation. I emptied the musky old bottles one by one, greedily, by myself. I found myself replenished, eager for more. Three flowers left.

Rampant Colette, the rapacious *grande dame* with the grace to regard me still as a boy, though the crow's feet were there, albeit invisible with foundation. We romped. Never before had I romped. I felt like a puppy. She was huge, this woman; catastrophically huge. She offered me an arid landmass to clamber and I keelhauled myself on her vigorous bulk. I who, when first mate on the barge or juice extractor by the pool of the dewy-eyed girl, had felt dignified, self-possessed and ... well, large, was dwarfed by this grandmother. Earlier, exactness, precision, the delicate clasp had been all. Now I needed to take a running jump, hold on for grim life. She, in her turn, toyed with me, flicking me about with able, coarsened hands. She ripped me to shreds, parts of my body were tattered and bloody after each encounter. But I loved it.

As I say, she was catastrophically huge and her heart, so deeply buried and imperturbable, gave a resounding click one afternoon as I tricked her into coming. Penetration had never done the trick; it was a slight thing, the licking of her nose with a feather that tripped the alarm, as I bobbed in and out of her like a sewing needle, but it was too much ... and that was that.

He was angular and stark and, I grudgingly admit, my next Japanese flower was quite like my earlier self. I was of an age to appreciate a retrospective narcissism. Like that portrait of Isherwood, the wryly salacious glance in the mirror at the younger you. I let him, as my poor dear Colette had let me, cross and re-cross the continent I had drifted into. He rummaged amid what he would turn out to be, but with reverence. I was his temple, his monument, and he came to me to pray. As pigeons spatter on Nelson's column, he brought forth his juvenile cockfuls of phlegm onto me. I took the tribute well; cleaned my roughening edges on his purer lines.

Naturally when his grandfather copped it, he cleared off with the inheritance. He got money. The lucky sod.

And my last ...

We are always told to keep the best to last. In a meal, with the courses and deliciously aromatic, steaming constituents arranged before us, the least wasteful, most sensible among us save the best till last. Michelangelo on the barge knew this. He ate the prawns in the cocktail last of all. I laughed at him; stole them before he ever got that far, from under his intense Mediterranean gaze. I could never bear puritans. Luckily I never had one for long.

But my first flower would have appreciated what Grandfather bequeathed me last of all.

The last flower trembled between my fingers above the water's eager meniscus. It was a crushed, violet rose. Genet would have approved. I held my breath; number seven. I didn't dare tear through the empty book's pages to check that I hadn't counted incorrectly. I opened my hand and the petals fell.

It was a rubber band.

When I finish scrawling this, on these pages thickened and stiffened with canal water, chocolate smudges, fruit juices, wine stains, come from men and women ... then I shall press them back together. Perhaps the book, its spine thwarted with fattened leaves, ruptured by sated desires, will refuse to shut. To this end I am going to use the rubber band. I don't know where it may have been ... but who cares? Just look where this book has been. Michelangelo was right, in a way, in that woolly head of his ... rubber bands do 'come in'. This one will stretch a coherence across the messy infusions of my life.

And one day, most probably quite soon, I shall stretch it. Stretch it open ... like foreskin, like hymen ... and peer between the dark pages for the signs, the delicate rustlings between the sheets of more dried Japanese flowers, the ones I know must still be in there, somewhere.

JUDITH'S DO ROUND HERS

I'LL TELL YOU who I'm a fan of these days, and that's that Roseanne. You know that fat wife on Channel Four? I think she's dead funny. And it's like they say in the *TV Times*: she's a role model.

She's my role model now, I've decided. She gets away with it. She's not ashamed of who she is, and she tells people what she thinks of them. She doesn't put up with any old shit.

I was at work when I was reading this interview with her, the one in the *TV Times*. We keep them on the counter with the evening papers. Which means we have to stand there all week with the same old famous faces staring up at us. You can watch the weeks go by that way.

Last week it was Roseanne and I thought she looked dead glamorous. Well, she *is* dead glamorous for a fatty.

I'm not being nasty when I say that. She says she's a fatty herself, she admits to it and has a laugh about it. She's famous anyway and it needn't bother her now. She knows she's a fatty and really, she's made her fortune out of it. And I can't use it as a term of abuse anyway, because when the chips are down, I'm a fatty. Mind, it's got *me* bloody nowhere.

So all last week it was Roseanne's face staring up from the counter, and that's when I read the interview. It was quite interesting. She's had a hard life, actually, even though she's on the telly and that. I felt quite sorry for her.

I like a good read. Especially interviews with stars like that. When they've had a decently hard life, but everything turns out all right and there was stardom waiting just around the corner.

We get all the magazines with that kind of real-life stuff in here. So I can have a good flick-through when we get slack. I needn't ever buy the things. Which is a saving, really, because I think I'm addicted, sometimes, to showbiz gossip and chitchat.

No, that's not true. Some of them stars I couldn't care less about. Specially some of them younger ones. Pauline, who I'm on with serving usually, asks me who it is on the cover of *Hello!* or *Top Santy* or whatever, and sometimes I just can't tell her. Who are these people? Why do they think they're famous? I have to look to see what it says underneath their faces.

I couldn't tell you who was who on *Home and Away* these days. They all look the same to me. And *Neighbours*. Now at one time I could have told you everyone in that, and everything what they were up to. But now . . . They've chopped and changed actors and that so much, I've not got a clue. So I have to look at the names under the faces.

Pauline still follows both, so she knows more than me. She still asks me to read the names out. Tell the truth, I think the lass has trouble reading. She squints up right close at invoices and stuff. And she's only just out of school. I've told her – I've had a lot longer than she has to forget everything what they taught me!

Anyway, yeh, so I read these chitchats and articles when we get a moment to ourselves. I mean, there's always someone in the shop. It's one of those shops where there's always someone coming in for something. We're handy and that's the point. Cigarettes – we're the place they come dashing out to and we've got an impressive range from your Craven As and your twenty-five-to-a-packet Royals, all the way up to your John Players and your Marlboros and even your Hamlet cigars. Top-of-the-range stuff we don't sell a lot of, but makes the place classier to have on show.

Or at least, so says Eric. Now Eric's the bloke who owns the place. He's a bit younger than me, in about his mid-forties I'd say, and he speaks a different language. He's been in business and done courses. I'd call him a greedy bugger, actually, but to give the bloke credit, he's turned this place into a gold mine. But it's for no one's benefit but his own. He serves his community, like he says, but it's also for his community that he's got broken bottles cemented round the wall at the back of the shop. What about that bairn – he was only a bairn – trying to break in round the back that night with his mates? Slashed all his legs, top of Eric's back wall. Severed tendons, the lot. And what does Eric say? Serves the thieving get right.

That's what I mean by a different language. Eric's forgotten. Now I know the family that kid's from. They live by us. They're not that different to what Eric's lot were like.

Yeh, I remember Eric from when we were at school. He was starting at the secondary modern when I was finishing. He lived by us. Like I say to Pauline, I've had the time to forget all-sorts from my schooldays, but some things just don't go. Na, they don't. Mind, Eric hasn't let on that he remembers me. I've said nothing to him and I won't do neither. Just let it go by.

I daren't think about all the water under that bridge, mind. I look a bit bloody different now. I was in my prime then. I was a bonny lass and they noticed me. Now I've – what's it they say in the slimming magazines? I've ballooned. That's it. I've friggin' ballooned.

So to Eric, I'm just like any of the other clapped-out, hard-faced, fat-ankled women round here. Just the woman behind his till he pays a pittance to.

Eric's got a wife a bit younger than him and she's not from around here. He's got a smart son who's up at the new university in Sunderland, doing business. Eric lets the kid run this place in his holidays for practice.

Now him, he talks a different language again, that kid. Alex, they call him. But he's got the same shaved neck, the same soft-looking smile and the same tucked-in arse that Eric used to have, bless him, so I forgive him bossing me about when he's down. Even if he is a short-arsed nineteen-year-old and really, on this town, I'm old enough to be his granny.

I'm a glamorous granny! They have special nights for

them down the Rec. What do they call them? Grab a Granny nights.

I went once, for a laugh, when I felt like I was looking a dog. I went to cheer myself up and feel younger. Sure enough, it was a load of witches in there trying to cop off with all these old fellers who'd come in a bunch from the British Legion over the road. You could tell they were from the British Legion because they wore them blue blazers with badges and caps and they reeked of booze.

Among that lot I was like a babe in arms. I was like one of them tarts off *Baywatch* who you never recognise but with all the tits and hair. Dead sexy like, at least, compared with the competition. All them hags in their mohair jumpers and thick tights. So I could have had me pick of any old feller there.

I'm not desperate, mind. I stayed around, flirted a bit and had a few offers, but I laughed them off. I pissed off out of there before some old sod took me serious. You have to cover your back.

I only went to give me ego a boost. Cheer myself up a bit. I looked a million dollars beside the grannies. Even in a room of British Legion men they still danced together and ignored them. I scooted out of that ballroom and into the ladies' and I cried buckets in one of the stalls. I don't know why.

When I went to splash some water on my face I met some young pregnant lass from the antenatal dance-class thing that was on the same night. She looked ever so bonny. Had I been to the ballroom dancing classes, she wanted to know. I think she was just making conversation. Dabbing a bit eye shadow on, close as she could get to the mirror over the basin. I think she must have had triplets on the way, size of her. She said I might enjoy the ballroom dancing more than the less formal Grab a Granny do's. The thing about ballroom dancing is that you'll always get a friend. I said I might give it a go. She smiled and went back to her class. Her common-law husband was keeping the mat warm, she said.

That was the last night I had out by myself. Now I make sure I'm with someone who'll pull me out of myself when I get maudlin. Which is usually when I'm on the gin, I must admit, and that's all I can drink anyway, because after a couple it tastes like pop and I've never really liked the alcoholic taste.

I said once to my husband – he's long gone, the first one – that that made me ladylike, me not liking the taste of alcohol. He said he'd like it more if I did get pissed more often. He liked me flat on me back with me mouth open. Oh, he was a pig and the one after him was no better, although we shouldn't speak ill of those who met with tragic endings.

Like I say, I'm a glamorous granny – I'm fifty now – but I'm not a natural one. What I mean is, I don't have any grandchildren. Most of the women my age I know have got them by now. But I've always been young for my age and they know that. I've still got jet-black hair. Dyed, of course, but it's a symbol more than anything.

So even though I ought to be, I'm not a real granny yet. My bairns show no signs of sorting themselves out in the kiddie department. That'll all come soon enough. There's no hurry.

Round here they hurry up. If you're not married and settled by the time you're nineteen, if you haven't got kids hanging round you all through your twenties, then they reckon something's wrong with you. That's not right. People make wrong decisions under that kind of pressure. I've warned my two not to get daft. You have to live with all your mistakes. And I think my two are being sensible. They're twenty-four apiece now.

Twins – not identical – a lass and a lad. The apples of my eyes. Andrew and Joanne.

Maybe it was the divorce and me having them on my own for those years, but we've made it different to how other families on this town work. I've drummed it into the pair of them, mind, but they understand all the same. They don't have to be like everyone else round here. They don't have to chuck themselves into something they'll regret. No one will think any worse of them for lagging. Well, they might, but their mam won't. And I *don't*.

I'm proud of them and will be even if they wait until

31

they're in their thirties to marry and give me grandchildren to fuss over and spoil and take to the park and stuff.

The reason you have to take your time is this:

Once you have the bairns and the council have given you a house and you have a job you think ought to last . . . then that's you. You're sorted out and, even at your luckiest, this will be how your life will stay. Until you're dead old and you're in the British Legion or you're a glamorous granny dancing with another glamorous granny down the Rec.

What I like to think I'm doing for my two – by telling them to slow down, to play the field, to think hard before doing what everyone else they know has done – is giving them a bit of space.

I want them to have chances. That's all I want. That's all any parent wants, I suppose, though you'd never guess, the way some of them round here shove their bairns straight out on the street, or take them out of school, or get them a job in the same factory as their dad. And that's if they're lucky, if they have a dad. That's no life.

Anyway, yeah, that Roseanne. She's had a hard time of it by all accounts. And you can tell. Although she makes you laugh and stuff – eeh, I nearly pissed mesel' one week, there was summat on, I can't remember, but it was bloody funny – you can see in her eyes that she's had a bad time really. It's always in the eyes. There's a sincerity in eyes.

You can never see it in your own eyes. Only other people can see it for you. Only, they aren't always up to the job of seeing the hurt in other people's eyes. Yet you have to rely on them. Mind, you don't want just anyone seeing into you. That's like broadcasting all your business.

It's funny, mind, how when you look in a mirror you can never see your own hurt. You might feel – I don't know – wounded or whatever, shat upon, but when you look in a mirror your eyes are suddenly bright and glassy and smiling just as mine were when I was being glamorous and young for me years at Grab a Granny night.

That's daft, though. As if anyone – especially a woman – can hide stuff from herself.

32

On the cover of this stack of *TV Times* Roseanne's smiling and advertising her new series. They reckon she's lost weight and she looks pleased with hersel'. She's got a new hairdo but I can see what's in them eyes and she's had it up to here, poor cow.

Sincerity.

I'm putting on me anorak round the back at the end of my shift. The staff room is tiny and it's full of all the breakages ready to go back. I tell you Eric's greedy – he wants his money back off everything dropped on his lino. There's smashed jars of pickles in the staff room and it reeks of vinegar.

So I'm zipping up me coat and crunching a pickle when Eric comes in with a full carrier bag. He gives us a smile like he knows summat I don't. Since he's the boss that's usually true, like, and I worry that some day he's gonna just give us me cards and that'll be the friggin' surprise. But the night he just gives us this filled carrier.

'You might as well have these, Judith,' he says. 'You've most prob'ly read them all already, but they're left over and I can't do nowt with them.'

I look in the bag and there's all this week's unsold magazines in there. *What's on TV*, *Top Santy*, *Just Seventeen*, the bloody lot. Well, I'm not too sure whether he's taking the piss or what, so I just shove it under me arm, collect me things, say good night and then I go. I know for a fact he can usually get a few pence for leftover magazines, so I decide he must be trying to be nice to me. He gives us a silly little wave from the back door.

I reckon it must be like that male menopause he's getting. I read about it and he's the proper age.

The proper age! It's not right that he shouldn't still be twelve. The age he was at first when I knew him.

He's looking tireder just lately. But he's all right 'cause him and his younger wife are off on a holiday next week anyway. Second honeymoon. They get about. Florida, he reckons. They'll visit the place with the killer whales and Disneyland. Not that they've any bairns to take. His son

Alex is looking after the shop next week, that's why he was telling me all about it. Besides showing off, like. I had to nod and say how lovely it sounded and how I hoped it kept nice for them and all the while I was thinking I'll have to put up with that kid again. In his little suit.

It makes no difference, really, though, who's in charge when I'm behind the till. Alex won't usually order me around unless his tarty little girlfriend is down to visit. They drive around in this big car of his. The roof comes off like they think they're in America. Sometimes all I can wonder is whether he's got owt in his trousers like Eric had back then, and I bet he has. He's the same sort of good-looking short-arse like his dad.

But I shouldn't even be thinking about the boss's son's trousers. The lad's over four years younger than our Andrew. Doing well for hisel', mind, whatever you say about him. My Andrew doesn't drive. He's had no one to teach him, no one around to do that, no dad. I don't drive. I think he'd be . . . not timid, but too *careful* behind the wheel of a car.

There's so many things to watch for. With your gear sticks changing and mirrors and looking at the road ahead and stuff. He'd be letting every other bugger get past first. You have to dig your heels in, push your nose in, get in there. I've told him. His mam knows that much. Our Andrew's not one to push hisel'.

When I get in the house Andrew's already there. He knows that when I finish work I need to sit down a while and relax. It's a full day on your feet and it takes it out of you. I've started getting palpitations in the night in me heart. When you push your thumbnail through the skin of an orange to start peeling it – that's what it feels like sometimes.

Andrew jumps up straight away when he hears the garden gate rattle and he's opening the kitchen door, ushering me in like an old woman, and whipping the kettle on, gabbling on.

He's a good lad and I can tell by the way he goes on when I come in that he's pleased to see me. He's had no one to talk to all day and this stuff comes pouring out as he picks our mugs off the tree, wipes them quick with the tea towel and pops the bags in the teapot. He doesn't work. I can barely get a word in edgeways.

I sit at the kitchen table and pull the ashtray towards me, smiling, listening. I can hear the telly's on in the front room, playing to no one, burning up pounds. The telly's on all day long in our house. It's dear but it's not just for the programmes. It's for the psychological glow.

It's children's BBC, all thumping music and excitable presenters. Andrew's turned the sound down before running to open the door to me, I can tell. He doesn't like me to know he watches the kids' telly. I can see why, a twenty-four-year-old young man. He'd feel daft, I reckon. But I can't see why he shouldn't watch it if that's what he wants.

It's all very sophisticated these days. As far as I can tell, it's all sex. And kids today learn all they need to about life and the facts of life from *Neighbours*. They cover every issue and more. Everyone on *Neighbours* has been married to everyone else, one time or another. That's why I get confused with it. Miss one episode and you've missed all-sorts. You'll have to struggle to catch up. Sometimes I think it's very true to life.

When I used to watch kids' TV with the twins when they were small, it was all puppets and animals. They wouldn't have that now. Now it's virtual reality and what have you.

Coming in from work, then, I smoke and rest mesel' and let Andrew make me tea. I can't smoke at work. Not even in the staff room because we have what Eric calls our delicatessen counter. He means the fridge unit with the cheese and that in.

Eric wants our place of work to be a healthy environment and that son of his is even more fanatical. Alex is a bit of an albino, he looks like someone's gone over him with a potato scrubber. Those pink eyelashes. If I've had a fag on the way to work and Alex can smell it on me breath, he's turning his nose up straight away like I've farted or summat. Little bastard. I wouldn't care, but he's lathered in great big red spots. I wouldn't buy cheese off him if you paid me to.

My bairns never had spots while they were teenagers. Haven't got them now. They've the complexions of angels – like their mother always had. Mind, Joanne spoils hers with all that make-up. She errs a little on the orange side, does Joanne, yet she won't be told.

'Mam, man,' she'll shout at us, and she gets dead riled at owt like this. 'Mam, man, your day is over and gone! Fashions have changed and nothing you can offer me in the way of beauty tips is any use. If I painted mesel' like you say I'd be laughed out of town! Face it – you've got an old woman's face and I've got a young'un. I have to follow young women's fashions!'

And that's how our rows about make-up end. But on my mornings off I watch *This Morning*. I know how today's young women get themselves up to go out on the town and that. Not to mention all the magazine articles I've flicked through. You can't tell Joanne, though. She doesn't realise how much the seventies are back now. Why, I was in my thirties in the seventies. Pale lipsticks and blue eyeshadow – I couldn't have been trendier then or now.

What our Joanne doesn't see is that she's still in the eighties. What with her frizzy highlights, her tangerine face. And God, but that makes me feel old! My own daughter in a fashion time warp already at the age of twenty-four. She's peaked her peak and all she can do is wait for the eighties to come back round. Probably when she's fifty.

Andrew is winding the pot up, poking a spoon in to mash the teabags. He's using all his concentration and the hot mist ruffles through that fringe of his. I reckon he'd get a job with a haircut but you can't say owt. Not because he'd bite my head off like Joanne would, but because he's too sensitive. I've given up criticising Andrew. His face crumples up like a paper bag and he looks at you like you've just said the worst thing in the world. Like he can't believe how cruel you are.

I think I've over-mothered him. I worry he's not had a

proper man's influence over him. But if he had it would only have been some silly sod making him wear a tracksuit to play football and stuff when he didn't want to. Who's going to blame me when I say my heart goes out to sensitive boys? What's wrong with it if I've said it's all right that he never went out much to play? That he drew pictures or preferred to read? Or that now he watches kids' TV instead of having a job?

'It's a grunge thing,' Joanne said when I said maybe Andrew could get a job with a haircut. She was on her way out one night – dressed like something out of Bananarama, but I kept me trap shut. 'And that's why he cuts holes in his jeans.'

'He *cuts* holes in his jeans? I thought they were natural.'

'Mam, man,' she said, about to slam the kitchen door. 'Sometimes you're so naive.'

Ay, I reckon I *am* naive. Because Joanne's definitely up to something these days. Something that's not just going out with her mates of a night. She's up to something with someone I don't know and I haven't a clue what it is. But I know there must be something wrong with it. Otherwise she'd *say*.

All the power's with her now and she's making me wait to find out. Only Joanne can make this storm break. And break it will, I reckon. Me and my family are in for a rough ride again. Joanne has a real tempestuous streak in her. She's even more of a rebel than I was. She's got my genes, only worse.

Well, we'll see. She'll tell me in her own sweet time. Or maybe I'll get it out of Andrew in the meantime. I know the twins share everything and for some things they keep their mam out. That's only natural. Children need their own spaces.

He's poured the tea and he's holding out my cup, giving me a look. That's 'cause I've lit me second fag and I'm enjoying it even more than me first. Andrew doesn't like me smoking. When he was five he said I should stop because otherwise I'd die. I think he'd seen summat on the telly. Joanne thought that was funny.

'When you die, do you want burying or cremating?'

She asked me this again and again. I didn't want to say anything because I thought it was morbid and it would give them nightmares. Eventually, I was ironing, and she asked me once too often.

'Look, Joanne,' I snapped, 'when I drop you can bloody well *eat* me if you like.'

Her jaw dropped in delight. But behind her, Andrew was horrified. Then he wailed and wailed and we couldn't get him to stop for hours.

In those days Andrew would always be standing just behind Joanne. He shuffled round after her like she had him on a string. They were like that till she left school, at fifteen. She went to work, learned how to be a receptionist. She's been in hotels, motels, the equestrian centre.

Andrew did O levels and went on to do his As but he finished early and just stayed home. It wasn't that he couldn't do them. He's got the brains. More brains than anyone I know. More than anyone round here. I reckon it was the competition that got to him. It was all competition and he's not that sort. He's too good for that. He doesn't have to compete, Andrew.

I take me tea and curl me fingers about the mug. It's warming. April and it's freezing out; still looking like snow.

Eric won't turn the shop's heating up beyond the legal requirement. Have it too warm, he says, and we'll have every dosser, every scruffy old bastard in off the streets, keeping warm. He's probably right but I still curse him when I'm freezin' me tits off on me pins.

I blow on the tea and take another drag.

'I wish you'd try again, Mam,' says Andrew.

He's got an almost girlish voice. A soothing sound, chalk drawing on soft stone. I can't be angry or irritated with him. Not often, anyway. His voice broke early when he still looked like a little boy. One morning he came downstairs and said something and the sound shocked us both. We both thought it was his dad asking for clean socks, although I don't suppose Andrew even remembers his dad. Since then,

38

he's changed that booming voice, made hisel' sound softer, on purpose.

'Try again?' I ask. But I know what he's on about.

'The patches.'

'Bugger them.'

'You could get used to them.'

'Oh, yeh.'

'They say they work.'

'So do fags. Those bloody things don't cost any less and when you pull them off they *hurt*.'

'But I don't want you to die, Mam.'

'I won't die.'

'Yes, you will.'

'Look, man, Andrew, will you stop interfering? It was all right saying this when you were five, but you're twenty-bloody-four now, pet! Look, I *won't* die!'

He looks at me. We sip our tea for a bit. Then he starts up again, flinching as if he thinks I'm gonna smack him one.

'I don't want you to die early. I don't want you to die before you can say you've had a nice time. I don't want you to die thinking it's all been hard work. I want it to get better for you first.'

Sometimes . . .

Sometimes he can say the nicest things. And that's the pay-off with having sensitive sons.

And maybe some time soon I'll give the patches another whirl, just for Andrew. It *might* make me live longer. I might get to see Andrew's children, my grandchildren. When they come along. I can change my habits. Showbiz stars do. That Roseanne lost loads of weight. They printed a photo of a pile of pats of lard, the equivalent of all she lost. She says she feels much better on it. I don't know if she smokes, though.

The next thing for me usually at that time of night is wondering what we should have for tea. I've never liked cooking much and by the time I get in on nights I can't really be bothered.

I remember frying up chips for the kids, winter nights after school. These were the years before oven chips, which only started in 1980. My home-made chips were always either too limp or too hard. A pale yellow and they sat in puddles of grease on your plate. The kids ate them slowly, dutifully, doused in tomato sauce. Which separated out into floating red blobs in the cooling fat. Like I imagine blood cells to look. Or a lava lamp working.

I wished then that I could cook better for the bairns and I wished that I could learn. But who is there to teach you? On a limited budget, not much time. Where do you go for perfect chips? And I'd sit and watch the bairns be good, forcing every last bit down. Then one night Joanne got a burnt one stuck in her throat and great fat tears came rolling down. Her face was all puffed up.

'I'm sorry, Mam. This is horrible. I can't eat it.'

And she looked so ugly and sad that I started crying too.

The 1980s began with oven chips being invented and we'd wrap them in newspaper to make them taste even more real. Also in the eighties there were other things, making mams' jobs easier. Pot Noodles – they came along and you could pretend, in your own front room, that you were camping out on some adventurous holiday somewhere.

Once, when we had my second husband, we *did* go on an adventurous holiday, to a caravan in Robin Hood's Bay, and we took twenty-four Pot Noodles with us, one each for each of the nights, trying every flavour. The front of the caravan was all windows and at teatime we'd leave the canvas blinds open to watch the sun set behind the cliffs and some nights we'd be eating Chinese, or Indian, or Mexican.

We never had pizzas until 1986. It seems like forever. Suddenly the local free papers had adverts for deliveries. You'd wait an hour after phoning on the spur of the moment. Then some lad would arrive on his bike, carrying the boxes up to your door, grinning in his leather rider's gear with his helmet on top of your boxes. Golden rounds of flabby garlic bread, cans of pop and lettuce leaves in tin-foil dishes. A treat we routinely surprised ourselves with every Friday night, coinciding with *Dynasty*.

For a while everyone was in padded shoulders, we all had

clumpy jewellery, and the men rolled up the sleeves on their shiny suit jackets.

The eighties were the twins' teens, my forties, and between us we managed to shovel on the weight. My husband then sold second-hand cars and by God, he was a big feller. I'll tell you about this some other time, but it was on that holiday to Robin Hood's Bay that we lost him. Swimming in the bay he went bobbing out away into the North Sea, never came back. It was terrifying and horrible, but somehow peaceful, too, to watch him, just like floating away. Like a whale put back out of captivity. That *was* about the time we all started going green. So we never finished our holiday properly – our first since 1976 (That gorgeous summer! I remember Lake Ullswater rimmed with cracked, parched mud, us eating breakfast, boiled eggs dipped in salt in the heat) – and we never finished all our Pot Noodles off. Had to bring them back with us. They're still in a cupboard somewhere.

These days the twins both cook and, as I say, we're all green now, aren't we? Healthy eating is the watchword round here and they're trying to convince me, but it seems a faff-on to me. I couldn't come in from work to clart on with garlicky things and what have you – salads. I'm too old to change all of my dog's tricks. I piled on the pounds in the eighties and I reckon they're here to stay for the nineties. Mind, the twins have shed their puppy fat. They did when they were about nineteen. They try not to, but I catch them sometimes, turning up their noses when I bake big cakes or rustle up a nice fry-up for tea. They'll neither of them eat baked potatoes or cheese on toast or crisps or Mars bars at midnight any more.

So it's a surprise tonight when I start to think about what to cook for tea and I go through on my way to the loo and, in the dining room, I see that it's all been taken care of.

Behind me, in the kitchen, I hear Andrew snigger softly. Pleased with himself at my gasp of surprise.

He's put on a lovely spread. He must have spent the whole day baking.

And I forgot! It had clear gone out of my head.

Tonight's the night of me soiree.

Andrew hasn't forgotten and he comes into the dining room to see me staring at his handiwork. He puts his arms around me and gives me a big hug, saying, 'The water's on, so you can have a bath and get yourself ready. I'll bring you a gin and tonic. You've an hour or two yet before your guests arrive.'

My guests! How could I have forgotten?

Tonight's the night I play lady of the mansion.

And our Andrew has done us proud.

What really snags me breath and makes me think, Ah, bless his heart, is that he's done everything like I used to do it for their birthday parties when they were small. Cupcakes in pink and brown icing, chocolate fingers, bread buns in half with red salmon forked neatly on, and some with my own special blend of tomato and egg, mashed together to a delicate rose colour. And half grapefruits, stuck all over with cocktail sticks – four bristle on plates all around the centrepiece – and on each stick there's pickles and pineapple and frankfurter bits, cubes of cheddar. The centrepiece is a Victoria sponge, oozing a livid mix of strawberry jam and cream. Its top is soft with sprinkled icing sugar.

And nowhere to be seen – not even on the sideboard where he's set out the cans of lager, the bottles, bowls of nuts and crisps and three fresh, shiny ashtrays – nowhere is there any of their healthy foods. There's nothing here that me or any of me friends and neighbours won't know how to eat or what to call.

I'm sitting in me bath with a gin and a cocktail stick of nibbles. Pink foam riding up over me nipples and I'm easing away all the aches and pains. I've got Tamla Motown playing out all around me. Our Joanne's a whizz with owt electrical and we've got four stereo speakers in the top corners of the room. At the time she put them in, standing on a chair with a screwdriver, I kept fretting because I thought it might be dangerous with all the steam. Like we'd all be getting shocks in the bath. But as it is, it's safe and bloody marvellous. I love to lie there, soaking in me bubble oil with Marvin and Tammi. The world is just a great big onion.

I've got a range of different bubble oils. Christmas presents last year, Boots' Natural Selection, from Andrew. Little bottles inside a wickerwork hippo. Tonight I'm in Fruits of the Forest and it's lovely.

I need to relax tonight. Have I mentioned yet the reason I'm having me soiree tonight?

God, I can't believe I forgot all about it! Lucky our Andrew's not daft.

Ay, the reason I'm having me mates round tonight. Wey, they're not all mates. Some of them are just neighbours.

You see, I'm not going to all the trouble and expense of playing the glamorous hostess just for the fun of it.

This night's Wednesday night and it's Wednesday nights Elsie and Tom come round.

I'm flicking through me frocks, head stuck in me wardrobe. Time's running out and I'm fucked if I can find owt decent to wear.

I'll slather mesel' in *Tendre Poison* and wear me heels and it's funny when you do that for a party in your own house. You stand taller and it's kind of formal and everything in your own rooms looks a bit different.

Wednesday nights Elsie and Tom come round after the Rainbow Gang finishes. Tom runs the Gang for the kids in the Methodist Church on the next estate. He looks like Dracula and he's had some trouble with his nerves, breakdowns and that, but Elsie says he was an architect when he was younger, before she knew him, but they laid him off. She's out of work with him.

They're not married and they come round menacing people. They've got God and they tell you the same stuff again and again, sitting there from six to twelve at night. I can't just chuck them out, like Joanne says I should. They don't mean anyone any harm and they're not malicious people. They're just daft. And they're company, even, sometimes, when Joanne is out at night and Andrew is upstairs, reading and that. Bloody boring company, mind.

A couple of months ago, Tom flipped. In the middle of their Rainbow Gang he was meant to be umpiring a game of indoor rounders, but he'd gone missing. Elsie was worried. She can't handle sixty of them scruffy bairns all by hersel', so she sent them all off on a kind of treasure hunt, looking for Mr Tom. One of the scruffiest – 'I patted him on the head and I could feel the nits squirming under me hand!' – found Mr Tom in a cupboard. He was crouching by himself in the dark. Elsie had to phone the Casualty blokes to come and talk him out.

Next time she came to see me it was alone. She was dead upset, so I was embarrassed because I'd been pretending I wasn't in that night. I'd turned all the lights off and the telly, kept quiet and waited for her to go away. I'd forgotten to lock the back door and she just came in! I felt like I'd been rumbled. I just said I'd had a migraine and had had to switch everything off, lie down.

She told me all about Tom. He was in that big place past Spennymoor, three bus rides away, and she was visiting him every afternoon, even though the doctors had asked her not to. They probably felt the same as I did about her knocking on the door. She bangs like a kid – bang bang bang bang bang. Demanding attention for a scraped knee or sweets or summat. Not an adult's knocking at all. Adults knock little tunes on doors. They don't sound desperate.

Tom was in this place, a big old mansion in its own grounds with deer and that. Pretty, but they don't put you in there for nowt. Elsie was saying to me, 'It's not a place for, you know . . . mental cases. Mind you, there's a bloke in the bed next to Tom who thinks he's Jesus.'

They let him out after a couple of months. I reckon they realised it was *her* they should have put in there instead. Bad depression, he was supposed to have had, really bad depression. I've known more depressed people these past twenty years or so than I dunno what. As soon as they invented a word for it, bang – everyone had it. I suppose

44

they invented the word about the same time they invented the pills for it. And most people I know have the pills handy. For either calming you down or pepping you up. No bugger's in the bloody middle. Nobody floats easily between.

Tom looked a lot better and more cheerful the next Wednesday he came round here. Elsie was wary about him, as if he was gonna freak any moment, and she kept jumping up to use the bog.

'Me bladder's back,' she said. 'All inflamed. I've got to dash back and forth all night these days. I know you've just had your settee recovered.'

I was bloody horrified. Woman of her age! She's fifty if she's a day. Though she's got that scraggy ginger hair of hers in bunches like a bloody schoolgirl. I reckon that's for Tom. I reckon he must be kinky or summat.

He was brighter than he's been for months, holding out the posters the kids had coloured in that night at his Rainbow Gang.

'That little Jeff,' he chuckled, shaking his head. 'Look! Poor little thing's gone and coloured carefully between all the lines. But he's done the whole thing in brown!' He tutted. 'By, some of the kids round here are underprivileged. They've not half got narrow horizons.'

Now that little Jeff he was on about is from over the way from me. He belongs to Fran, a friend of mine, but I wasn't going to say anything.

Elsie beamed at Tom. 'Tom's bringing colour back into all their lives.' A thought struck her. 'Is that why he called it the Rainbow Gang? Hee hee hee hee!' That stupid bloody laugh of hers.

I was looking at the posters. Tom the ex-draughtsman had designed them. A loaf of bread and some writing. I asked what it said.

Tom sighed. 'It's meant to say, "I am the People's Bread." But my "I" came out too elaborate, like. Now it looks like it says, "Jam the People's Bread."'

'Hee hee hee!' went Elsie again, but I could see Tom didn't

think it was funny. His eyes were hard and that was scary, I thought.

'Silly bugger!' Elsie slurped her tea.

'Elsie,' he warned.

He'd stopped her swearing, smoking, drinking. These past few years since she's known Tom and the peace Jesus brings her she's been a different person and a very different Elsie to the one I remember. And I remember Elsie from 1976, when my first husband worked down the icing-sugar factory with her husband and she worked in the canteen. There was nowt pious about Elsie then because 90 per cent of the time she was a prossy and pissed out of her head. That's why sometimes it gets me back up to hear about My Lord this and My Lord that and My Lord the other from Elsie. They're not even married, the pair of them. Yet they wouldn't hurt a soul. It's just that sometimes I can't face another night sitting hour after hour, listening to their same old crap. So, like tonight, I decide to put something right in their holy bloody path. I decide to throw me glad rags on.

These'll do.

First off it's Fran and Jane and daft Nesta turning up, on the dot of six o'clock. Fran wants to help with any sandwich-making or table-laying. Jane makes a beeline for our Andrew, who talks to her politely and takes the ladies' coats, and Nesta starts helping hersel' to the cider.

The lasses are all dead glad to be here the night. It takes a lot of planning for them to get away from their kids. Luckily nearby we've got Liz's old house. She was a neighbour who moved away, but her way-out daughter Penny has set up a kind of squat for all her weirdo friends. Penny's good with the bairns, so odd nights like this, their squat becomes a crèche. It's ever so handy, really, and I've had a look in – even though I've got no young bairns – and I must admit, for a squat it's immaculate inside.

Fran's having trouble with her husband who's drinking still and she's telling us all about it as she looks for something to be of help with. But I'm distracted 'cause there's banging at the back door again. I yell to Andrew to put some music on the hi-fi and then there's more guests arriving – the Wrights. They're a dirty, smelly family from by the garage but, as I say, it takes all sorts and this is a party and they're friendly enough. Then it's the Kellys from over the flats, back of us. Jane was reckoning on they were heading for divorce and she had her beady eye on the husband, Mark. He's a skinhead, tattooed head to foot, arse to elbow, by all accounts. Jane doesn't have a man. She went a bit doolally last summer and ended up doing a nude fan dance on her roof one Saturday morning, but she's all right now. I dunno how she climbed up there without owt on.

Anyway, the Kellys seem happy enough tonight, coming in with her mother Peggy and some young bloke she says she lives with, across town. I'd bet money it's her toyboy, although she cracks on he's her houseboy. Ay, right.

Andrew's put on Elton John in the living room and when the place is filling up nicely, 'Don't Go Breaking Me Heart' comes on. It could be 1976 all over again. When I was getting me divorce and every now and then I was going proper wild. Everyone's getting a canny bit to drink and having sausage rolls and that. That tattooed bloke even grabs me for a bit dancin'! Whey, everyone knows me round here, working in the shop, like.

Then there's Jane's mam and stepdad, Rose and Ethan, this old bloke with a wooden leg, coming in, and then our Joanne, back early for my do, from wherever it is she's been. She gives us a peck on the cheek as that tattooed Mark whirls me round and then she goes over to get Andrew to pour her a drink. High-class, our Joanne, she likes her drinks mixed proper. Won't touch a can.

And then at half past seven there's a knock at the door I recognise. Bang bang bloody bang. Just when, ordinarily, I'd be settling down happily to *Coronation Street*. You'd think they were doing it for badness. Someone I don't even recognise is opening the back door to them. By now the house is heaving with invited and uninvited company and Elsie and Tom shuffle in looking mortified.

'Is it someone's birthday?' asks Elsie when they eventually find me.

'Get some cake and some drinking in,' is all I say and scarper elsewhere, leaving them to it. Someone's blowing one of them party kazoos and streamers have appeared from bloody nowhere. Honestly, round here they don't need any excuse to get arseholed.

'Mam, it's the phone!' Andrew tugging on me arm. 'The police are asking us to quieten down.'

'Tell them to haddaway and shite. They never get on to the Forsyths over the road when they're up all night ravin' and stuff. They can bugger off.'

Andrew looked sick at this. He hates confrontations, even over the phone, bless him. He's never been one to stand up for his rights. I grab the receiver off him.

'Is it the desk sergeant you've been talking to?'

Glumly he nods.

'Right.' Andrew winces just before I yell into the phone. 'I don't care who's phoned in to complain, you toerag, but you can fuck off! It's only 'cause you're not invited.' And I slam the phone down. I had to shout louder even than I meant to, because of all the noise of the party. Good! Deafen the bastard.

Andrew looks scandalised. 'Mam!' Behind him Tom is returning from the toilet, and he looks sick. 'Mam, you can't . . .'

'Ah, shurrup, man, Andrew. It's only yer dad.'

'But Mam, he was tellin us – the neighbours had been phonin' to complain.'

'But all the neighbours are here now.'

'Except the Forsyths.'

'They'd never . . . !'

But I'd not put owt past the Forsyths. Last month one of them was up for biting off someone's ear.

At the moment, though, I'm still thinking about Andrew's dad, even though I don't want to, but talking to him just then, just when the party was reminding us of the seventies and all, well, it seemed sort of right to me. It brought lots of it back in a flash. Mind, faces round here have changed. Even the ones that were here in the seventies, they've changed. We're all a good sight more haggard. Time's been having its revenges and all our bairns – the bairns who in the seventies were in their polyester Incredible Hulk T-shirts and pigtails and played with Bionic Men and Sindies – they're all grown up themselves now. And I mean, really, God knows what they're up to. They don't tell you owt.

There's a lot of drink at my party. The whole night comes to me in snatches and bits I don't recall. At one point I'm drinking out of a paper cup for some bloody reason, and I'm sitting on the stairs with that Peggy, Sam's mam, and all I can think is, but I never bought any paper cups! The party, Peggy's saying, dead seriously – and we're the best of mates by now – the party has run away on its own steam and we must be ready for anything to happen.

Peggy starts some long, daft story about a baby left in her care since last Christmas. She reckons it fell out of the sky in a shower of feathers, but she's more pissed than I am and, quite honestly, I'm starting to think that everyone at my party is bloody daft or mad. And suddenly there's Elsie tottering out of the downstairs toilet, pissed as a hatter and clutching a bottle of Pils.

'Hee hee! I've got the Lord in me!' she screams at us on the stairs and she looks friggin' manic.

Quick as a flash Peggy yells back, 'Ay, and I've had him in me an' all and he was crap!'

We piss oursels laughing and Elsie doesn't get it, which makes it funnier. She staggers down me hallway and falls flat on her face. We cackle a bit longer, waiting for her to get up. Which she doesn't.

The next thing I remember sees us all sitting round Elsie's cooling corpse on my Redicut rug in the living room. It's past midnight and the music's off now. Like a bloody vigil. Some bugger's found me emergency candles and everyone's sitting round Elsie's body, watching Tom stooped over her. For some reason I'm the only one talking.

'If we have a power cut,' I'm saying, 'one of you buggers

is gonna buy me new candles. If I'm caught short in a blackout . . .'

And then I look at Elsie, along with everyone else.

We all look shattered, in our party clothes. No one looks as white as Elsie. She's got an even dafter look on her face than usual.

'I wouldn't give her the fuckin' kiss of life. I'd kiss me own arse first.'

Yes, I know. I'm ashamed of it all now and all the lasses have reminded me of the horrible details. Mind, we can still have a laugh about it.

I can see everyone gasping and watching Tom rub Elsie's hands and breathe warm, foisty air into her face. Honestly, it's better than the Paul Daniels show and Elsie's that Debbie Magee, his tart.

Then she's got a pale-blue glow all around her and she sits up like a fuckin' zombie.

Whey, I scream liked I've never screamed before.

That starts some of the other lasses off, who think I've seen something they haven't seen. Jane's nearly hysterical by the time Elsie has coughed three times in a row and started to sing in a really high-pitched voice that Ken Dodd song, 'Happiness'.

> 'Happiness. Happiness.
> The greatest gift that I possess.
> I thank the Lord that I possess
> the greatest gift
> and that's happiness.'

Then she passes out again and Tom cries out at the top of his lungs, 'Praise the Lord!'

No one round here's that religious, so no one adds anything to that, only dirty Simon, Sheila's husband, pipes up, 'Are we all doing turns then? Cause we've got wor karaoke tape we could bring round for yers, if yer like. It's a fuckin' hoot.'

So they do and the party's going on till dawn.

Joanne and Andrew haul me up to bed eventually, while

it's all still going on. Through the floorboards I can hear Jane belting out 'I Will Survive' and then 'Agadoo' with Nesta and then she comes up with Fran to check on me and I've been sick on me dressing table.

Apparently, before I fell asleep, I was crying and saying that I wanted Eric – me bloody boss! – inside me again like he was when I was seventeen and he was twelve.

I'd never say that unless I was paralytic and I reckon I was because I never made it to the shop for work the next morning.

THE FURRIER THE BETTER

HOW WAS I to know she was married to the man who owned my lighthouse? Adele will never forgive me, but I had no choice. I was coerced. I was oppressed. But Adele won't listen to reason. She of all people should sympathise with a pure and simple case of oppression. But still she won't forgive me for doing what the wife of the man who owned my lighthouse made me do. After all, she neglected to tell me they were her *parents*.

I wouldn't care, but it was all Adele's fault in the first place. She made me go on *Kilroy* with her for moral support.

That began the sequence of events which culminated in the appearance of furry emerald crocodile skins on the bowed backs of every rich bitch in this country and beyond. Adele holds me responsible for all of it. Because of me she has even more high-street targets for her buckets of pig's blood.

But let me backtrack. Let me fill you in. I want to savour each fragment of my decline. At the time I was barely sensible. In my current penury I can take it much slower and convince myself that there really wasn't anything else I might have done.

Well. Here goes.

Adele was my best friend and she campaigned. I was going to defend her immediately by saying she wasn't your average campaigner with dreadlocks, Alsatian on a string and irony stuffed uselessly up her arse, but fuck it: she was. She was still my friend and, occasionally, when she could afford the train and boat fares, would come out to visit me at my lighthouse.

It was extreme north. You know all those frostily exotic place names they mention on radio shipping forecasts? So exotic you could never visit them because you know for a fact that these counties, these regions, have no *ground* to speak of? Well, I lived in the thick of those. I was a small pinprick in an ocean of thrashing, icy chaos and I loved it.

Boats passed by occasionally, passenger ferries which hunched their shoulders and nudged through the storms. Mostly Scandinavians off shopping for the day on Tyneside where things were cheaper. I'd be out walking on the wet black rocks surrounding my magnificent home and there'd be rows of bright blonde heads on a ship going past, waving their *Top Shop* carriers at me. They speak ever such good English.

Would it be immodest to call myself, a humble lighthouse keeper in the middle of nowhere, a sex symbol? Well, it's over now so it doesn't matter. But those Scandinavians would wave at me. Hold their new frocks up over the ship's edges, under their chins, for me to admire.

And sometimes the ship would briefly dock and out would tramp Adele with her Alsatian and little haversack, come to stay a couple of weeks. Off the ship would sail again.

All I saw otherwise was the fishing boats. I was meant to train my incredible lamp, beam its bluff ebullience in the fog for the fishers' benefit. But those rude bastards always know exactly where they're going. I was virtually redundant. Not that I would let on to the owner of the lighthouse. He thought I was being quaint. Only recently I realised that his wife made him keep me there. She was after the fabulous furred crocodile, well before I even became aware of its precarious existence. Me and my lighthouse: we were set up.

When Adele came she would bring lots of booze, mung beans, vegan supplies, and a whole heap of pamphlets tortuously written by the permanently irked. There was always some cause or other.

On one visit she said to me, 'I envy you being out here alone. Because you can hide your head in the sand from what's going on in the real world. The horror on our streets.'

Adele knew all about the horror on the streets. She gathered up money for marine life in shopping malls, sprayed paint – and latterly pig's blood – at fur-draped matrons, and took Cup-a-Soups to prostitutes at midnight.

I tried to point out that actually, I was doing the very opposite of hiding my head in the sand. Rather, I was right in the thick of it. I stuck my neck right out, in the wilderness, isolated in my splendid tower, and took what the world at its most tumultuous might chuck my way.

She scowled. 'And that's very male. Stranded up here on your massive prick, you've no idea what the real world's like.'

I suppose she was right. On *Kilroy* I caught up quickly with what people were like. And it was awful.

Your average television discussion programme is a hot-house. They trawl in the relevant punters, perch them uncomfortably under steaming lights and send in one ringmaster with his microphone and whip for an hour. It's always uproar and he has to shout to drum up coherence and decent telly. Make the topic anything you like and there's always uproar. Oddly enough, our show was especially loud. Furs get them hotter under the collar than most things. Teeth and hair flying that morning.

On one visit Adele came skipping along the rocks to hug me, the ferry with its hoard of Norwegian shoppers flapping their goods and receding into the mist behind her. 'I'm only here for a few nights,' she exclaimed. She had hennaed her hair, I noticed, with too much tea. Because of the sea spray as I kissed her I could taste Earl Grey on her forehead. 'Then I'm going back to the mainland and you're coming with me. We're going on the telly.'

Years ago, before I elected to stick my head in the sand – or raise it above the humdrum clouds, whichever way you look at it – and before Adele was the kind of legitimate campaigner who gets asked to go on TV programmes, we were lovers in college. It was the sort of affair that no longer seemed appropriate once the years of glamorously damp terraces, Mexican rugs, alfalfa sprouts and piss-weak beer on a Thursday night were over with. Thinking about it, though, Adele is still in precisely that culture. She never left it. I did. After graduation I threw out my little Indian hat with mirrors on it, and my long mustard cardy with holes in it, and fucked right off. So maybe there was a future for us after all. Maybe that's why she kept on visiting. We'll never know now anyway. In a dank cellar somewhere in a university town this very moment, Adele will be lighting an incense oil burner and cursing my name.

Which is Terry, by the way.

And all of it because of the green furred crocodile.

Furred to sustain it in the wild North Sea. It had evolved for itself a harsh winter coat, fur like that inside a kettle or the pipes lining the interior of my lighthouse. A tough, evil-smelling fur. God knows why they want to traipse about with it on their backs anyway.

But they bought it. They queued in their thousands for a snippet of my crocodile, earlobe-to-ankle coats, even shoes.

The first I knew of the crocodiles was when they went round murdering seals on the west side of my island. I did like watching the seals gambol, but they began to die off at an alarming rate. I found them strewn around like badly punctured, bald tyres. Poor things! I thought at first, ironically enough: hunters. But the dead seals' little suits were quite buggered up in these attacks and a hunter would never do that. And then I thought: *Jaws*. Instantly I saw myself as Roy Scheider, alone with only an oar to defend me, slipping down the sinking ship's deck into some ghastly, jagged maw.

Then, with my golden telescope, from the top of my tower one morning, I observed the killing of the last few seals. Crocodiles. I could hardly credit it.

They came in packs of five, like Woodbines used to, calling out to each other, it seemed, as they waddled up on the rocks, surrounding their pathetic prey. Who could never run fast, bless them. Seals lollop and attempt to bounce. Chuckling nastily, I was sure, the crocodiles herded them up and took a swift bite out of each. They did it for fun, it seemed, nonchalantly and with a distinct cool. Like blowing up a crisp packet and exploding it with a clap. Their armspan-wide jaws would clash and the seals went pop.

I watched in, as they say, horrified fascination. The crocodiles were jewelled, and rightly proud of their hardy opalescence. Before each other they preened their shimmering, roughly coated skins and they shook their fur free of water, like dogs. Peering closer, I saw thick, matted green beards and disturbingly elfin ears.

Resolving never to tell anyone about this spectacle – I didn't want film crews making nature documentaries on my rock, drinking all my booze – I quickly rerouted my walks to avoid a confrontation with my new neighbours.

On those rerouted, rather more alert and shifty walks, I would find the odd steaming heap of green shit. And tufts of moulted emerald fur. But I wasn't going to let evolutionary anomalies chase me out of my home.

I forgot about them – almost – until Adele arrived to ask me to go on the telly with her. I went out to think it over and took her Alsatian, Foucault, for a quick jog around the rocks. And one of the great hairy bloody things ate Foucault.

'He fell in,' was all I could tell Adele, proffering her his snapped chain.

'But he can swim!' she sobbed.

'Yes, but there's all-sorts in there,' I said darkly. I was hinting broadly at industrial waste, knowing that Adele would understand and come out of her shocked grief with a habitual blast of righteous indignation. The loss of Foucault, however, was a terribly cruel blow, and I saw that I would have to return to the mainland to appear on *Kilroy* with her, just so she could get through this testing time.

So, as we left my lofty home on the ferry, over the churning grey waters, I watched behind and toasted poor Foucault with a gin and tonic. I toasted my wonderful lighthouse also, sorry to leave it even for a few days. And below, I knew, beneath the frothy white wake our ship was drawing, the crocodiles were screaming with laughter. Underwater their outrageous hair would stand sinisterly on end, and they'd be pulling Foucault's wishbone for a laugh.

I was torn, I must say.

Under the hothouse lights, when you're going out live to three million homes, when it's ten in the morning and everyone's shouting themselves hoarse in a raucous carnival of vox-pops, you have to know where you stand. There's no use if, when the man with the microphone comes your way to ask your opinion, you look indecisive and go, 'Um . . . er . . . well, I can see both sides, actually . . .'

There's no time to be equivocal. Not on daytime TV's fast lane. You can get run over by an outspoken member of the public quick as a flash. You have to be openly biased and play out your part. That involves being nice as pie to each other in hospitality and then going for the jugular on the studio floor. One bloke was telling Adele she was evil for chucking pig's blood at people. That was when the camera was on him, but afterwards he was horrifically smarmy and waltzed her off to his hotel. *And* she had my tickets and wallet in her bag. That's how I came to be stranded on the mainland, but I'll come to that.

I couldn't be partisan. I was only there for moral support. I was sitting next to Adele but when they zoomed onto her for her opinion, she was incoherent with rage (she had just been called evil), and I got asked instead for mine. And I didn't know. I went, 'Um, ah . . . well . . .' And everyone groaned.

Does living at the top of a beautifully whitewashed lighthouse make you a weak-willed and irritating liberal?

But I could, I could see both sides. When Adele was frothing at the mouth because they said she was wrong for attacking fur-wearers in the street, I thought, Well, she is a bit daft, really. That freezing day she was arrested for it, so cold that her blood iced over in its bucket, she threw it and someone lost consciousness. I couldn't condone that, not even for Adele. Not on live TV.

Nor, however, could I condone the ones they got on to defend the furriers' trade. A nasty gaggle of trumped-up scarecrows, jangling their bracelets in the front row like Jimmy Savile's fan club. They all talked in measured, reasonable tones about their right to wear what they liked, about their rights as human beings to be tolerated. One of those in the front row was Monica. While the others ended up shrieking, losing the arguments and the phone-in vote, Monica remained as placid and sweet as a viola.

On the monitors above us Monica's forehead shone. She wore heavy dark glasses and her skinny neck stuck straight out of her voluptuous coat. 'I bet it's a man,' Adele hissed when the camera went on her near the start of the programme. From where we sat we could see only the back of her head, but her voice rang out, defending her rights, filling the studio.

'Do you wear leather shoes and eat meat?' Monica asked someone dressed just like Adele. The other campaigner shook her head violently, looking ill. 'Well,' added Monica, 'I bet you have a dog. I bet you have an Alsatian. Do I infringe your right to have a dog? How is your Alsatian different to my coat?'

Beside me Adele burst into tears.

I was comforting her and wishing I'd stayed at home when I saw that the microphone was being waved under our noses again. They wanted Adele's sobs for public consumption. At last I was irked enough to vent a little spleen. I suppose I came on as exactly the kind of annoyed boyfriend that gets up any woman's nose, defending his tearful girl. But what else was I meant to do? I said that Monica was a heartless bitch and I'd like to see someone wearing *her*.

She threw back her shiny head and laughed fit to make the microphone feed back.

'And another thing,' I ranted. 'You lot think you're so smart with your bloody mink farms and leopard-hunting and God knows what, but where I live I see something unique in its natural habitat. Every day I see fur that you'd spit feathers for.'

It was a hideous mistake. Monica stopped laughing and turned to look straight into the camera. Disconcertingly, she was smirking from the monitor right above Adele and me. Adele, too, stopped sobbing and looked at me.

'What are you on about, Terry?'

And, still going out to the nation, I announced, 'Great big bloody hairy crocodiles on my little island!'

Then came a swift commercial break and I was mobbed by a flurry of furry grandmothers.

By the time I had fought past those liver-spotted claws and their brandished chequebooks, I was back in hospitality and Adele had been whisked away by the man who accused her of being evil.

Monica advanced slowly from the opposite corner of hospitality, slugging back the free wine with a Sobranie decorously on the go. Recognising her elevated rank, the others drew apart, giving her access to me. Monica's green eye-shadowed eyes narrowed with indistinguishable lust and menace.

Oh, dear! I don't want this to sound misogynistic. Here I am making Monica a vamp, Adele just dopey, espousing the virtues of living in a phallic monstrosity, my own terror of crocodiles in fur. But I'm sorry. This is social realism. The seals were all ladies and I thought they were lovely. Until the crocodiles got them.

So Monica came up and plied me with drink and vile-smelling gold-tipped cigarettes. She explained that she'd been longing to meet me and had known that one day she must.

I was, I admit, quailing. And the floor manager kept appearing, wanting to shoo us out of hospitality. 'How did you know about me?'

'Why!' She smiled. 'You're the strapping young man who works my darling husband's lighthouse, aren't you?'

I was dumbstruck.

'What a coincidence we should meet here today! Was that your little friend making an emotional display of herself? You see, I was hoping to meet you soon anyway, because I already knew about your crocodiles.'

'You did?'

'Genetic engineering, dear. I have a contract with some industrialist chaps. They've been running this little number up on my behalf for a few years now. You're ideally placed to fetch them up for me. Honestly, my dear, you've no idea what it cost me. Chanel looks positively off the rack compared with paying off the big boys.'

'You paid someone to *make* hairy crocodiles?'

She blew smoke at me. 'Darling, it's called postmodernism. You may literally live in an ivory tower, but you must have heard. It's all the rage, dear.'

And then she bunged me a wad of notes to round up her precious mutants.

For once I was under no illusions. The phone in hospitality rang at my elbow and I snatched it up as she went on smoking. It was Max, my unctuously superior boss and – as I had discovered – her husband. He purred into my ear as she watched, telling me I had to give her what she wanted. It was more than either of our jobs was worth. Then he was gone.

'I'll send a whopping great helicopter over tomorrow night, when it's dark,' she continued smoothly. 'It'll have to be under cover of darkness in case the papers are watching.'

'But . . .' I stammered.

'What?' she snapped.

'Adele's taken my tickets, my money . . . I can't get home anyway, until I find out which hotel she's gone to.'

'Oh, you are tiresome!' She glanced around quickly. 'Luckily I enjoy sailors.'

'Pardon?' But I'd never been a sailor. I dressed that way, but it was a pure affectation for the sake of wandering about on my rock.

She looked at me as if my stupidity turned her on. 'I'll pay your fares and things if you fuck me in my furs on that settee. Max can't bring himself to do it with a wild beast.'

She wasn't particularly wild. But the fur got up my nose and made me sneeze all the way through. It was bizarre, like fucking a strategically shaved bear. And I, poor, bereft, isolated lamb, hadn't done anything of the sort since the days of Adele. Being clasped between shiny thighs as I screwed by rote and stared at that forehead, I was stunned.

Into submission and I was sent out on the streets to return to my rock and dutifully round up the crocodiles.

The next day darkened and waned on my rock sublimely as always, though I wasn't to know this was my last night there. I was busy at work, getting ready for the distant whirr of helicopter blades.

In my befuddled state I had dreamed of what I thought of as an infallible plan. At least it had seemed that way on the queasy ferry trip, during which my prick had throbbed in self-pity until it spied its lovely, welcome sister, my lighthouse. I had decided to dress myself as a seal and *lure* my prey.

Hours I spent gutting the miserable carcasses and stitching them – like a perfect sailor – into one huge and, I hoped, convincing creature.

I tried it on and I must admit I looked fabulous. I still wear my sealskin occasionally, and flop about on beaches the length and breadth of the country. What else ought I do without a job? We workless, heterosexual men have to do something for kicks in an age which is 'postmodern, darling'.

So off I went, the following night, stumbling on my cumbersome tail across damp rock. What now? I wondered. Do I shout, 'Come and get it, boys'?

I remembered the sight of the seals that gambolled in shallow waters and on the shingle. I emulated that for a bit, thrashing the water to make ripples that the beasts might sense. That was when I found I quite enjoyed it; the rancid stink of the fur's uncured interior and the tang of frozen salt water. I came inside my second skin a couple of times and, while thus distracted, heard the crocodiles snorting as *they* came.

They almost got me. My eyeholes had slipped in the post-orgasmic panic, yet still I ran like hell up the beach.

They pounded through the surf on their stumpy little legs;

fifteen, twenty, thirty of them. Luckily I couldn't see them, but to hear them was enough.

In that instant I thought, Yes! Kill them! I agree! Much better to wear the bastards and swan about in society than let them run about innocent lighthouses wreaking havoc! Their venomous chops clattered and slavered hungrily at my scraped heels.

And like the lights of heaven, the lighthouse shone brightly down upon us. I was, once again, stunned. Then, as the crocodiles all peered together up at the tower, we saw that a helicopter hovered beside it and had discharged one of its company into the lamp room. She waved at me. Adele.

Adele was training the light down on us as the crocodiles circled me and began to look nastily suspicious. We've been fucking set up, one gnashed to his neighbour, and was right. And so have I, mate, I thought miserably, preparing to be devoured.

But down swept the helicopter and Monica herself appeared at the open hatchway, mink stoles flapping and forehead glinting in the night. With a well-modulated scream of triumph she picked off each of the beasts with a poisoned dart. She took them all and never disturbed a hair on their heads.

I passed out and, when I came to, found myself dressed as a seal with Monica bending over me and Adele busy all around, helping to sling the creatures into the back of the helicopter.

'My daughter.' Monica glowed with pride, and I passed out again.

Now that I'm out of a job, I sometimes come to stand on this particular beach – dressed in my neat little suit, although it's shabbier now and smells awful – and I look out at my precious ex-sanctuary.

On the promenade every now and then you see someone being the height of fashion, glowing the chemical green of a furred crocodile. Usually a woman, but affluent queers are getting into the same kind of thing. The animal-rights lot are up in arms. But they can't decide how natural the things were in the first place. It's an ideological problem. It's postmodernism, dear.

I was lucky, really, to escape only unemployed. They actually wanted to silence me. Monica gave me a speculative glance, when they had me trussed up under house arrest in their opulent front room. She'd always wanted a sailor suit. But Max looked nervous at that point and they let me go. I wasn't furry enough, it seems. Every one of my hairs had dropped out in fright that night and that's another reason – besides disenfranchisement and simple fetishism – that I like to wear my second skin.

Maybe Adele will come back, catch me up one day, and explain her political qualms about this. I may have been in a phallic ivory tower, but I think, surely, her own ideological position needs to be clarified a little? I mean, how *can* one chuck buckets of pig's blood one day and cull crocodiles the next?

I miss my nice simple tower. Life was so easy when I was a sex symbol, master of all I surveyed, with only the seals and Scandinavian shoppers to please. Lighthouse keeping's a dying art, fuck it.

EMMA'S SITUATION

OUR LANDLORD DIDN'T visit very often, and when he did he would tell us about his once giving Lulu a lift to Leicester. In the days when the boy she was with looked more like Lulu than she did. When she was a *rising* star. He told this story so he could look at Emma and, with an ingratiating nod, say that he hoped it wouldn't be too long before he saw *her* on the telly, as he had seen Lulu, two weeks after he had driven her to Leicester, singing 'Shout'.

Emma would flap her arms about, shake her head and lower her eyes murmuring soft deprecations, still giving him her best profile. Then he would bustle out with a little giggle, clutching his rent cheques. 'Lulu!' Emma would exclaim as his car was heard roaring back off to Leicester, and I would be reading again.

She straightened her rubber gloves and went back to cleaning the toilet, each time. Our landlord always discovered us like this, me reading, her cleaning the toilet.

It was part of our little ruse for renting this tiny canalside house that we pretended to be, of all things, a couple. Whenever the rent was due, or the soot-encrusted wiring fused, I would grimly submit to one of our landlord's visits and gamely feign heterosexuality. Emma played along like the fine actress she thought she was and would drop in the odd mention of my incorrigible untidiness. Just like a man, she'd chortle, and toss her hair.

Our landlord would be upset, she reasoned, to find that we weren't a couple. Not that it was in the contract that we were meant to be. Not at all; it stated plainly that we occupied two rooms and that each room had its full complement of accoutrements. But when the landlord showed us round he giggled, sidled, nudged, and made it quite plain that he thought we looked good together. Emma put her head on one side and fluttered her eyelashes. At that point I barely knew her but, looking back, should have know then that she was off her head because those eyelashes fluttered out of synch with each other. A bad sign.

Two memories of that day we looked round the house by the canal and signed the contracts:

Standing on the black iron bridge spanning the canal, staring into the sheets of brown water, wondering if I could stick her for a full year. Next to me she was in four-inch platforms, rocking on the wooden slats, draped in black net. We were waiting for the landlord to arrive from Leicester. We really needed this house. I was being thrown out of my old house the next day, and Emma's friends had let it be known that they weren't into having her in theirs, either. Until the previous week I had been going to look at this place with a boy. But there had been a scene, a skirmish, a deconciliation. As a consequence he dyed his hair red, I stopped reading his poems, and we both made alternative arrangements. My alternative now tilted her wide-browed, triangular face towards me, pouted and purred, 'I think that's him there, with the carrier bag. He's a dwarf, look.'

In those platforms she walked like a camel's front half. Her leggings were beige, to exaggerate the effect. It meant that she reeled helplessly and harmfully through the narrow passages and pasteboard rooms of the empty house. By the time she hit the biggest room, at the top, she reined herself giddily in and declared that we would both be taking it.

The dwarf and I exchanged a mild glance. These middle-class girls knew how to get what they wanted.

My second memory is of turning the mattress in the biggest room. It had been designated mine, since it had a double bed and, as Emma hissed at me while we examined the bathroom in the extension out back, *I* was sexually active while she most certainly wasn't. Then, without turning a hair, she raised her voice to ask the dwarf if he minded Blu-Tack on the flock?

So in the biggest room the landlord suggested we turn the mattress. I don't know why, really; we were checking the furnishings, testing the inventory of bits and bobs. The wardrobe door had just creaked and sidled itself off its hinges, banging against the wall, so I think he was out to distract my attention. When we looked at the mattress either side, he sadly surveyed the stains and clicked his tongue. 'The last resident was a lady,' he apologised, taking us both for men of the world. Then he explained that she had been on medication, and that was why the wardrobe was broken. The lady routinely flung herself at the furnishings.

We had a kitchen window which stared straight out onto the bridge and we could watch people coming back from town. As the first few weeks went by I laid a neat row of emptied green bottles along that sill, then across each scrupulously wiped surface, the top of each dusted cupboard, and around the skirting boards. I had Pre-Raphaelite postcards stuck to each kitchen cupboard door, and my ghetto blaster permanently by the draining board, belting out Liza Minnelli's greatest and Philip Glass's *Low Symphony* morning, noon and night. It was fabulous.

The overspill of paperbacks from my room and the living room appeared in tall piles on top of the telly (whose tube had already blown) in the kitchen's corner where the stairs ended. I worried sometimes about the pages being impregnated and warped by the cooking fumes, but, since each book was a slim volume of something or other anyway, decided it wasn't a problem.

There were a lot of fumes, though. Each bottle in those careful rows represented a meal cooked at some elaborate length by me. Since I taught at irregular hours, I would often start cooking at two in the afternoon and dinner became an increasingly baroque affair. I set myself into a pattern of cracking open the latest Bulgarian red and plunging into the first glass as the oil began to shimmer and boil in our wok. The glasses were a moving-in present from a very dear friend so, I reasoned, it was a waste not to keep them in almost constant use. I had lovely teatimes stirring the wok with a fag in hand, Liza shrieking out 'Maybe Next Time' again and again.

Emma eventually pissed me off because when it came to her nights to cook she did some terrible things. Rehearsals went on late or, when they ended on time, they had drained her too much. She produced chicken casseroles for which the contents were tipped altogether into one dirty pan and allowed to broil till they emerged in a grey broth thickened only with splinters of bone.

And the washing-up! On went the Marigolds, but for Emma, washing up meant turning on the cold tap and dangling each item under the flow for a few seconds, then tossing it willy-nilly into the nearest cupboard. Looking in the cupboards later was just distressing. Slimy wet plates and saucepans still caked in grease, scabbed in sauces and rinds of dead pasta.

This was the girl, the eldest of the many offspring of her house, who had had to take charge of the housework in holidays. Her father was a stern Indian Catholic who knew where he wanted his daughters to be. And that was in the kitchen, by the playpen with his youngest son, while his wife recovered from nervous exhaustion on his Bupa insurance. I met him when we first moved in and he brought Emma's clothes, her cheese plants and a Hoover in his car. All the way from Buckinghamshire, so he must be fond of her, I thought, despite all her late-night rantings about her evil father. He took me gently aside in my nice bright kitchen and warned that, at the end of the academic year, he wanted his daughter sent back to him *intact*. I laughed in his face at the time.

Later, when we stopped eating meals together – after a particularly rushed concoction of Emma's into which she had slipped an entire jar of garlic granules by mistake and still expected us to eat it – dinner became an even more elaborate charade of careful planning. When I let Emma do hers first, however, I would go to the cupboards to take out the dripping, filthy utensils and crockery and just about quell the nausea in time to hear the actress's decorous retchings and splashings from the bathroom. Which put me right off cooking again.

Emma would appear jauntily pale in the kitchen, unashamedly wiping her mouth on her sleeve, belch bile fumes at me and ask, 'Aren't you eating tonight?'

I tried to get in with my cooking before she did. Which was easier those nights she had her friends round for tea. They liked to eat late and on the floor in the living room, where they played Wink-Murder and talked about their respective senses of isolation. I would come downstairs to find the curtains pulled down, chairs overturned, dirty plates strewn. Everyone looking guiltyish. In their hands Wink-Murder could turn rough. And once I found one of the Adonis queens from theatre studies whom Emma had befriended, standing in the centre of their seated circle in nothing but a towel. Emma was looking straight up at his polite bulge in front and enjoying the game, popping soft mints into her mouth.

I guess I was making a nest and lining it with the stuff I wanted around me. At first, even though it was late in the year, the light came slanting yellow and clean through the house all day. When I filled the place with flowers, tucking them into jars of coloured glass and two by two into wine bottles, they shone.

Maybe I should have let Emma have more of a say in the way it looked. But she paid very little attention. The housework she did do was bathroom cleaning, sporadically and with great aplomb. This never prevented me finding the occasional spattering of vomit down the toilet bowl, the slovenly beige bulge at the U-bend's mouth.

Emma showed off the house and – to begin with – her housemate to her new, theatrical friends. They weren't *real* theatrical friends. They were, for the most part, pinched-looking, oddly dressed, nice middle-class boys and girls who, in order to be given second-class degrees, were required by their third-rate department to perform in about four plays apiece and perhaps have a stab at directing one. Emma worked hard at befriending them so that they would give her parts. She wined and dined one called Simeon to get to be Sally Bowles in *Cabaret*.

These friends looked at me askance. Especially the hugely fat girl called Clara whom Emma took as her extra-special friend. Clara was prone to feeling isolated.

I remember one night with Emma sitting on the floor grasping Clara's vast hand and squashing it, almost singing as she told her, 'Oh, but Clara, I care, I care, I care about you so much.'

Clara's long hair was pulled into two poodle bunches, dyed fuchsia, and they seemed to have winched and contorted her face into a spiteful grimace. That chemical green, furred coat she wore was slumped across her shoulders like a blanket on an accident victim. And Clara was staring at me almost accusingly; 'But do *you* care? Do you?'

Those small, beady eyes squinted at me and I looked back.

At that time, what I relied upon each morning to rid me of my fags-and-booze-induced headaches was my bare feet hitting the cold kitchen lino. It usually did the trick, but some mornings they nagged on. The day that Emma recommenced early-morning opera practice in the cellar was one of these.

She'd only started again because our morning routines had been forcibly altered at my insistence. Until then she had brought me coffee and the post in bed. Sitting up and being pleased, I was often mildly shocked by her rather sinister innocence in unfolding my bedclothes and climbing in beside me for five minutes. I put a stop to that in the end and the opera began in earnest. As I told her, she'd thank me for it one day.

This morning, though, as I fussed over the coffee-maker and slopped water over the side as I filled it, she appeared out of the cellar, banging its door hard behind her, and confronted me with a determinedly autonomous breeziness.

'I need to know about *The Tempest* for a seminar today,' she said, clutching to her chest a scarlet Mozart score.

Watching my toast char gently, I told her all about Caliban, about monstrosity, about cursing in taught languages.

Two nights before I'd been in my room with someone and, in the middle of the night, we were overtaken by a giggling fit which, thinking about it afterwards, I realised Emma must have heard.

That evening she had held one of her dinner parties and when my new friend and I came home we found them eating Smarties from dessert bowls and stirring themselves to dull conversation.

Emma walked in on my friend and me kissing in the kitchen and looked startled by us, so we just went to bed early. I admit now that I was making myself look a fool with him anyway. My flesh creeps to think of how I *clung* that weekend. Literally, the pair of us standing on the bridge as we went home that night. When it seemed risky and fun to snog in full view of town, neither side of the canal. How, unlocking the door and unmindful of being heard by those on the other side, I had told him I could really fall for him in a big, bad way. At the time he urged me to keep that to myself and in retrospect it wasn't just to keep it private.

Later Emma said, 'Didn't you even think about how I would feel, seeing you kissing in my kitchen?'

In the middle of that night, though, after three, after Emma had seen her last guests off, after they had filled the house with black smoke from making popcorn and we had watched it seep under my door, we listened to Emma clump her platformed way up to bed, slam her door, and then we started to laugh.

We imagined Emma's dinner-party repartee. How she was having the builders in. She was going to have her hymen knocked through. A darling little archway affair.

How she liked to have nice things around her. Living with a faggot was *so* convenient. She could do with two faggots, really; paint them green and stand them to attention either side of her darling archway.

So we laughed and in the morning, around nine, Emma kicked open the door and brought us coffee. The room was overly bright because my friend had tugged the curtains closed and they hadn't been secure enough. They were in a dusty heap on the floor and all the street, it seemed, could see into my room.

We were squinting as we woke and before we knew where we were, Emma had left the coffee on our respective sides of the bed and whirled out again.

We had slept without covers and I had found myself cupping his bollocks in my hand. An unconscious gesture I recall now with embarrassment, not because she would have seen it, but because he might remember it.

He went on a late train that Sunday night, never came back.

After an eleventh-hour shag I sat in the freezing station with a dribble of sperm tickling at my ankle, inching into my sock.

In less than three hours, I thought, he'd be back with his real lover, in another town, in the sunken bath he'd described to me, with candles nicked from the nearby cathedral lit all around him.

And, before he went, he talked about that commitment to the man with the sunken bath. I'd said something about no one's commitment to me, the bitterness easing out.

On the train as it pulled away he was reading the book I'd lent him. It came back a fortnight later in a brown envelope, without a letter, and Emma commiserated.

The week after he went she had another meal and invited me too, to cheer me up. I'd been looking depressed, apparently, and had shouted at her when she burst a bag of sugar on the kitchen floor.

Emma had been so shocked at my shouting that she ran to throw up, went out to buy two bottles of Bulgarian red and spent the rest of the night telling me about her father, how he'd forced her to the brink of suicide on numerous occasions.

When she was home for some religious thing that year, she wrote to me and said she was, at that moment, sitting on her packed suitcase, cutting off clumps of her hair.

'I am mutilating herself,' she wrote, in her distress.

To this meal she invited Simeon, who was directing *Cabaret*. He was pale with dyed black hair so dull it made his acne seem lustrous and healthy. He wore perfect white gloves and talked incessantly about Liza Minnelli. The girl he lived with, who looked uncannily like Liza Minnelli, was also there, discussing isolation with Clara on the settee.

In the kitchen, stirring her chicken broth, Emma hummed 'Maybe This Time'.

Simeon did a long monologue, later that night, about coming out and being fucked over by an older man who locked him in a room for a week. Really, he could only face the world these days because of the friendship of the girls he had met since.

I took the last of the Bulgarian red and watched as Emma and Clara took one gloved hand each and squeezed it, wringing their affection into him.

I went to bed.

Usually that meant whirling around, flat on my back, for an hour or more, until sleep slammed onto me like a lid. I would miss sex because it often filled that worrisome hour and prevented me from raking up each terrifying aspect the future liked to present.

That night I heard a rustle under the door. When I switched on my light, I saw that Emma had sent me a note.

She was confessing how much she cared for me. Said that we really had to talk. That she knew I was a man and that she wouldn't shy away from 'the physical act'.

Even though, I was thinking, as I tried to sleep, stunned, even though her virginity was displayed and dusted off before each surprised visitor to our house, like an especially posh coffee table they were invited to admire.

When I slept I dreamed I was pregnant.

72

At teatime the next day I spent three hours being sensitive.

I said I thought we were like brother and sister.

That although, yes, I had and did sleep with women . . .
no, I wouldn't be doing so with her.

I said that friends meant much more to me, as a rule, than
lovers. I'd had that said to me a year before, and despised the
person who said it. How easily it came to me now!

When I think of this scene – explaining patiently to Emma,
watching her tilt her cheekbones as if receiving successive
glancing blows – I see us sitting in an odd location on the
living-room floor. I have a good memory for locations, so
it must be true. We were sitting where a door used to
be, between front room and kitchen, the flowered curtain
between pulled back. Emma sat on the kitchen lino and
hugged her father's Hoover.

She gave me Lawrence's poems for my birthday with a nice
message about friendship. And invited Clara round for a
meal to celebrate my twenty-third.

I bided my time, thinking that, just in the nick, somebody
else would arrive to drag me out for an alternative. Somebody
else would leave a man with his own house and a sunken
bath. Somebody else would be catching a train, knowing it
was my birthday.

But Clara came and I heard Emma whisper to her on the
doorstep the reason for tonight's meal.

By midnight Clara was sobbing on the settee; Emma was
clutching her hand. Next year Clara had nobody to live
with, her friends had all made other arrangements and
she was consequently feeling – quite justifiably, I thought
– isolated.

Emma glanced at me as if asking, Can't she stay here?

As it happens she did stay that night.

It got so late and Clara had been so upset, we decided
that it would be a good thing for her to stay.

It got so late because they were discussing their parts. Clara
had been offered Sally Bowles – I was surprised, too – and to

ease Emma's rancour, she had been given Ophelia in Clara's *Hamlet*.

'Aren't we incestuous?' Clara grinned, her make-up smudged to frightening effect.

In Sainsbury's that afternoon Emma had confided to me that she thought Clara had lesbian tendencies.

'My God!' I said, picking out mushrooms.

'I don't know how to handle it.'

I tried not to laugh. I tossed the mushrooms into the trolley and dusted my hands down my jeans. 'Handle what, exactly?'

I once made the mistake of using the word 'cunt' in its literal sense in a conversation with Emma. In the kitchen where, at night, our wide window was like a mirror. Looking past me, she was pouting at herself and tilting those cheekbones and when I said 'cunt' she very nearly stopped sucking in her cheeks.

When Clara stayed that night I agreed to take Emma's room and lend them mine. Straitened on her self-assembled pine single bed, I heard them giggling. For a moment I thought they had actually decided to contribute to the lesbian continuum. I went for a pee and saw, through my opened door, that they were removing an Athena poster of a naked man from my wall. It had been there as a joke, really, that had played itself out.

'We couldn't sleep under *that*,' Clara told me, balancing on my bed, rolling him up.

The light came in brighter into Emma's room and kept me awake all night. In the morning they had already gone, to begin sitting in on each other's rehearsals.

After I made my bed I found that my letters had been read and strewn across the floor, along with several items of my more androgynous clothing.

There was fresh vomit in the bathroom and the coffee machine had been left ready to go, the morning's post propped up beside it.

Over breakfast I thought about what to cook that night and how to tell Emma we had to find new living arrangements. I have a good memory for situations, and most of those I have had and still remember are ones I am glad to have over and done with.

The difficult thing about breaking up the happy home would be explaining it to our landlord, the dwarf, who thought he had us on lease for three years. Until, as he saw it, Emma became as big as Lulu. In his eyes stardom and long residency were linked. He took Lulu as his model and saw that sticking at a situation resulted in success. And Lulu had been a star for more years than either Emma or I had been alive.

LAMINATING IDEAL MEN

SHE'D NEVER FELT safe behind a desk and look! Here she was.

She was running a gym, it was the job she'd always wanted, but the irony of it all, honestly! Behind a desk again, with the gym shipshape under her command, its rigging creaking in the salty breeze from the rowing machines and the step machines. Mid-morning saw her fiddling with a paperclip. The desk was empty apart from the phone and a little plant.

Trish gave a covert glance across the reception area to check herself in the mirror behind the coffee things. Andrew liked to offer coffee to customers. They were meant to pay, really, and there was a sign up but, he said, let them think they're getting something for nothing. They'll remember and come back. What we want is a nice regular clientele in our pockets. Butter them up with coffee, with free goes on the sun beds, anything.

She was checking her hair in the mirrored panels. It was a problem. Being in reception all day meant she did her own training at odd moments when they got slack. Sweating at intervals like that tended to make her hair go limp.

'It looks fine.' Helen was getting them two plastic cups of coffee. She bent to stir her sugar in, leaning over the wickerwork table. Some youth was poring over the body-building magazines and Trish watched him stare at Helen's body. She was all in Lycra again, a glossy indigo, and she looked just like one of those female body builders, one of the famous ones who still manage to be feminine, as they say. This physique of hers had crept up on Helen. She used to be plump, if anything, when she first started work here. Then – bang – one day she walks in in Lycra and she's like this, all toned and fabulous. Behind her back Andrew had scowled. 'That's all on *my* time, that. *I*'ve paid for her bloody body.'

'Your hair looks fine.' Helen gave her the coffee. 'Am I still making this too weak?'

'I think you've got the hang of it.'

'It's different to instant.' They sipped and Trish tested the potted plant on her desk for dust. Helen added, 'It's nice.'

'I think I should talk to the cleaners.'

Helen looked blank. 'When do we have cleaners?'

'First thing. Before you arrive.'

'Do you know, I never thought about cleaners before. I suppose it stands to reason.'

'Why do you think the place always smells of Mr Sheen?'

'That's it! *That*'s the smell. I've been trying weeks to work that out.'

'Mm. That's what it is. Mr Sheen.'

'Funny, isn't it? Once you've found out what a smell is that's really bugged you, then you smell it everywhere after that. I think smell is a really evocative sense, don't you?'

My God, it's true, thought Trish. I smell furniture polish wherever I go.

She had a small daughter, just about to go to school, reading aloud already, mind. Her knick-knacks, breakables and ornaments had been stowed away for a few years now. Used to her home environment being safely clutterless, unfussy, she compensated by polishing surfaces till she could see her own face, smoothing the rounded corners as if everything were chrome.

I'm a furniture-polish fetishist, she thought miserably. And only a couple of days ago she'd been worried about not doing her share in the house. Dave, her bloke, spent more time at home and most chores fell to him. That's all I do, really: run home from the gym at the end of the

day and whizz a duster over everything in sight. That's
my contribution.

And she thought about making love with Dave. Last
night's accusation that she somehow inspected him during
the process still nagged at her. It was true that Dave had
let himself go, though. He had slackened. But do I really
seem as if I'm checking him over, even then? My God,
he's alert and wary of my professional eye. Am I really
that bad? Now she was imputing a cynicism to his every
gesture made recently in her direction. When she licked
him all over, from head to foot. Christ, now it seemed
even to her that she'd been dusting him. Giving him the
once over with Mr Sheen. Licking him back into shape.
Poor Dave!

Native Americans they call them now, but we'd know
them more properly as Red Indians. Teepees, arrows, peace
pipes, all that. Well, apparently they're topping themselves
all over the place. The men, anyway, the young men, since
they're not in tribes or in the wilds any more, they feel they
have no fixed role. They've nothing to do. They don't feel
like men.

Dave was home watching morning TV. He liked to watch
the debates and that, keep his mind occupied, abreast of the
issues. Morning TV coincided almost exactly with playgroup
over at the council community shack.

And that bloke with Nirvana; shot himself. An icon for
a generation, they reckoned, though Dave had never heard
of him till he was in the paper. Said he was one of the
Blank Generation, whom Dave hadn't heard of either, but it
turned out he was part of it too because he was under thirty.
On the telly they said; roleless, overqualified, depressed.
Mind, Dave he had nowt for qualifications and he had no
job either.

He was a wonderful father.

When Trish came in bursting with energy and gleaming
with aromatic oils each evening, she kissed his forehead.
'You're a wonderful father!' The news would be on. Dave
could never quite follow what went on in Bosnia. It was as

if even wars conspired to block him out. He'd followed the Gulf War avidly and had even felt a real part of it. Doors were closing all about him these days.

Adverts. After the break, a phone-in on modern-day masculinity. Dave didn't like phone-ins; if it became heated they cut the caller off. Time to pick the bairn up.

'Pully push-downs?'

They were standing in front of one of the machines and Trish was showing a prospective member round each thing. At moments like these she was proud of all they had accomplished here. All these machines painted gleaming white, glinting chrome as they worked, the sweet tang of oil, of Mr Sheen. This whole place had been storage space for Fine Fare and Andrew had snapped it up. Useless, it had seemed; shelled out and grim. Almost like magic, they had given it form and function.

The prospective member shrugged. 'That's what the bloke at my old gym called them.'

'We have different names for different things at different gyms.'

'Does that cause problems?'

'No, because bodies stay the same. Now, have you been bringing the bar down to your chest or to the back of your neck so that you can hear the bones cracking?'

He gulped. 'My neck.'

'That's totally wrong. God, there are some real cowboys about! What you should be doing – otherwise you'll do your back in good – is . . .'

She was in the saddle, demonstrating and talking at the same time when Andrew went sailing past in his silver shell suit.

My Cyberman! She smiled, almost letting the bar go.

'Morning, love,' he called out.

'How's Sedgefield?'

Andrew was disappearing into his office with its mirrored windows and the prospective member was caught in his and Trish's crossfire.

'Just wonderful. On its feet and running itself. That's Phase Two under way!'

Trish said, slightly out of breath, 'He's just opened our second branch in Sedgefield this morning.'

'Really?'

'So if you drive – do you? – you can go there, too. We alternate days for saunas, so you could have one every day, but I don't think that would do you much good. Yes, Andrew's very enterprising.'

'I had no idea it was such big business, this game.'

'Oh, yes.' She nodded, working on the bar again. 'It is.'

The prospective member was watching a woman exercising her legs across the way, sitting down and slamming her knees together, stretching them apart again, her expression rapt, then startled.

'That's an abductor for your inner thighs,' explained Trish. 'Not very elegant, is it?'

Every time the woman opened her legs he could see what her T-shirt said. 'Thrill Me.'

'Keep going, Joanne!' Trish yelled. 'Think about being in the sun in a fortnight and getting that bum off!'

A surprise is always a good thing. It always does the giver good too, and so Dave decided to repaint their Laura's room. Pink. There was some left over from doing the downstairs hall. It was under the sink. He made the decision waiting outside playschool. He could have it finished by tonight. All finished, clean and ready for Laura's bedtime.

'Hiya again.'

One of the mums. She was fifty if she was a day, with hair bleached so hard, so mercilessly it looked made of seaside rock. He might stretch out a hand and just break a piece off. Her face was papery from a good few decades of smoking. When she smiled, that paperiness made her eyes look cruel. Trish had cured Dave. She tore up two hundred duty-frees once, after returning from Spain. She kept him locked indoors fagless one whole bank-holiday weekend.

The bleached mum grinned at him. 'Don't you wish they kept them all afternoon, too?'

He never liked to get into conversations here. It made him look too involved. He was here doing a favour, picking up the bairn. It wasn't a routine, he was just here every dinnertime. He wasn't part of the mums' set. Their fleet of candy-striped, dirt-mottled pushchairs, their squawling brats, their hissing at each other, their sucking on fags in all weathers. Dave didn't want to be drawn into their orbit and yet he invariably was.

'Yeah,' he said. 'Especially when you've got things to do.'

'Have you got things to do this afternoon?' Her voice had dropped a note, she looked side to side.

God, he thought, I know what's coming. 'Yeah,' he said. 'I'm doing up our Laura's room. Pink.' Sugar-and-spice pink. But the bleached mum's surreptitious glance was switching about again, as if she was gearing up to something outrageous. He knew what. That glance took in a certain gaggle of mums all too familiar to Dave, a set studiously ignoring him today. A set with whom he'd had doings in the past. They ignored him, but they were talking about him, he knew. Hiss hiss hiss. He sighed.

'I've been saving up the child allowance,' the bleached mum said.

They're late letting the kids out, he thought. It's gone right chilly. Shit, she looks her age! Guess what's coming next!

'That's nice,' he said. 'What are you planning to do with it? Go somewhere nice?'

'I hope so.' She was looking sly again, carrying on really shifty. Probably didn't know what to say or do next. Well, he wasn't about to help her out. He had stuff to do anyway. A room to strip and paint, a thousand stuffed toys to relocate and protect under sheets from spattered pink drops. He had plenty on today, thank you. Dave was a busy boy. First he had to find somewhere for Laura to spend her afternoon . . .

The bleached mum had gathered up her nerve. 'Them lasses.' She nodded at the group standing to one side, now

81

giggling among themselves, clutching at each other. 'Them lasses were on about summat yesterday . . . summat you do . . . that you've done for each of them . . . a service you offer . . .'

Dave tensed. Fuck! Word's getting about. A one-off first and then it snowballed. He'd never meant to let the numbers mount. This one was the oldest yet. 'Yeah?'

'Twenty quid?'

Five more than he'd got off the last one. He frowned.

'That's for an hour, so long as it's now and that you baby-sit our Laura till five as well, no charge.'

These negotiations over, the skills they could offer hung for a moment in the damp air. Right now! she thought. She hadn't been expecting *right now*, yet it made her feel sexy, really.

'All right,' she said.

Pull the curtains on the daylight, he thought. Do it quickly, as you'd rip off a plaster. Get it over with, then get onto the chores. You want to paint, paint, paint, paint, paint till teatime at least.

The shack's doors flew open and there was an eruption of energy, of small bodies pulling on anoraks, waving arms and crumpled, still-wet finger paintings. The kids tumbled out, sure of being gathered up, knowing whereabouts those who waited stood. Dinnertime. Dave hoped the bleached mum had something decent in to eat.

A big expense, of course, had been putting twelve TVs in the gym. Same thing in Sedgefield. Andrew never skimped. MTV was on continuously. Music all day, pounding in every room; it helped to get people addicted to the adrenaline rush. Andrew explained, 'We grease their chemical reactions with cheap music. It's all very scientific, it's all very primal and sexual, actually,' and he raised an eyebrow.

At his urging Trish had taken an access course in science. He had let her go part time to do it. It was all about nutrition and, as he saw it, a vital part of her job. She thought he was very kind.

'Sound's off in the main reception area.' Helen looked red in the face and cross. She'd been stretched up on her swollen, exercised calves to reach the suspended screens.

'What?' asked Trish and went to look.

Andrew had asked her if she wanted to go to university to do a science degree. Her! The best course was in Leeds, he reckoned. But it was part time. A hell of a run out. She'd have to think about it. What would it mean, what impact would it have on her job, on her family life? And was she brainy enough?

'There's no volume knobs.' Helen jabbed at one of the TVs. Trish had to agree. The volume must be controlled from some central point. Funny they'd never noticed before. The things just came on, busy and loud, each morning, went off again at closing. Neither she nor Helen was gifted on the technical side. It was people and bodies that they worked with. On the four TVs hung from the ceiling in the reception area Take That were dancing, spinning and flexing their torsos to silence. They didn't half look queer, Trish thought, dancing with no music on.

'I'll go and ask Andrew.'

These were Andrew's quiet hours in his mirror-windowed office. Helen tried to point out she'd already had a word, but Trish had vanished in his direction.

She grunted 'Harder!' as if by rote, thinking it the thing to say in the circumstances. Still, Dave complied and found himself concentrating only on fucking harder. There was nothing sexy in it any more, he was just fucking harder because he'd been told to. He was putting his back into it. Her back was rigid beneath him and each time he fucked their bellies clashed, then came apart with a fat sucking noise. Her rough hands were on his arse cheeks, stretching and pulling him, making him go harder, and his balls, he realised with a shock, were almost senseless and cool with nonchalance.

Fucking, he thought (and the thought was an old one he'd not had since his first time) was like being ironed. As if you're a crumpled white shirt. Imagine being ironed immaculately but someone leaves the collar bent up and rumpled. The shirt is taken down from its hanger and although mostly neat it feels vaguely dissatisfied and will do so until that collar is sorted. Now imagine the collar set upon by a scalding iron; crushing down on the errant spot, drenching the fibres with steam. This hotness plied around his cock, the focus of her body as a means to slip his foreskin wetly back and forth, trawling him closer to orgasm, all that was just like doing the ironing. And when he came it was with a brief, shuddering sigh like that given by the upended finished-with iron.

As he settled back, withdrawn, tugging the condom away and fiddling with himself, she stole one kiss. With the smoking she tasted like iron, like earth, and the used condom was cold on his shin.

She locked his office door from the inside and, sure enough, found him face down on his expansive, empty desk.

'I don't *know* how to turn the sound up on the bloody tellies!' he sobbed. 'It's usually automatic!'

'That's all right.' Trish sat down opposite him, patting his hands. 'We'll get someone in.'

'But Helen was looking at me like I was meant to know! Like I needed to know!'

'Never mind her. She never knew either.'

'But I should know! I should know how to turn up the volume on my own tellies in my own gym!'

'That's what you employ others for, Andrew. You're becoming a mogul. Especially with Sedgefield underway and everything. It's time for you to relax.'

He raised his head from the desk, his eyes gone puffy, to see Trish putting on her rubber gloves. 'Time for . . . ?'

Andrew's body was what he liked to call the male-model look. He used himself as an advert for prospective members: this is the look we can aim to give you if it's the male model you're after. There was no spare fat on him. He had the sucked-in stomach and pendulous wide tits everyone was after these days. He looked alert, almost rodenty with

84

alertness, and his streaked, thinning hair was slicked back for ease.

Every couple of days Trish would lay this cultivated form out naked on his empty desk. He would trust no one else with the job. From a small locker she produced unlabelled bottles of exotic muds and unguents that smelled foul but were packed with marvellous nutrients. And rolls and rolls of clingfilm. They were testing out this treatment for members, they told themselves. As the weeks had gone by, however, they'd decided that it was much too good for all and sundry.

She was very used to his body by now. Working here together, they were bound to get used to the sight of each other. The final revelation, flushed pink, toned up and still embarrassed, hadn't fazed her much. Still she hadn't touched him directly. She let him smear the first layer of greenish mud on himself. She was no masseuse. It was with that taut, squeaking winding sheet of clingfilm that Trish really came into her own. Lifting one limb at a time, she wound and wound the plastic about him, tighter and tighter. She could feel the heat trapped inside, squirming in his lathering of jellies. Andrew remained silent throughout the operation. There was the odd soft moan, maybe a supressed curse when she tweaked a leg hair.

Slowly, slowly, every inch was covered and he was a good 25 per cent bigger all over, layered like a lasagne. When he was immobile in the glistening, shifting crust of plastic and gels, Trish would examine her handiwork. His head stuck out at one end of the package wearing a curious expression. His face was scarlet but the inches-thick overcoat was a dull silver.

'My Cyberman!' She smiled at him, allowing them both their first show of affection this whole session.

Only once had she tried to persuade him. 'You might as well. You'd get it all for free.'

Dave supposed his eyes were beseeching. His Bambi look, she called it. He loathed it because he couldn't help himself.

'I can't do it,' he said. And he knew she thought he'd let himself go.

'We might as well take advantage of a free offer.'

Still nagging on, she came up behind him as he swabbed down the kitchen sink and the draining board. Dave threw down the rag. 'Look, I can't do it. I just can't.'

Later, calmer, he offered the excuse that he'd find it difficult, working out among other men who were eyeing up his wife.

'It's not like that – '

I know it's not like that, he told her, but even so, *I*'d be looking at you and that'd be no good for you working or me working out, now would it?

Trish shrugged. She only wanted him to get out of the house a bit. She thought he looked cooped up. He always looked as if he'd just woken up. She had suggested training as an alternative because that was what she knew. That's how you got out of a rut, and she knew that because it was her job. He resented her bringing this work home.

'I'll take the bairn up to bed.'

'Right. Dave?'

He looked at her. Laura's head lay curled over his shoulder as he hoisted her up asleep.

'You don't have to shape up for me, you know. It's for you, really. For your own peace of mind and health. I love you, you know, as you are.'

'Yeah, right.'

The truth was, and he thought it over later that afternoon as he started in earnest with the emulsion and white spirit, the truth was that he was unnerved. Other men unnerved him and they always had. He had never worked out why. It wasn't that he spent much more time with women, either, mind. So he put it down to his being a loner. Did the thought that everyone unnerved him make him feel any better?

When there were no women about, men were odd together. There were rituals of brashness and Dave felt excluded from these and therefore from whatever greater confidences were later tendered.

As he mixed his paint in Laura's room, Dave asked aloud, 'What do men say to each other when they're alone?' The words bounced off half-stripped walls. Curls of cartooned paper rustled round his feet. He'd spent three hours stripping already. Fucking therapeutic, mind. Drips of pink up his forearms from stirring too hard. He could still smell the bleached mum on him.

So what was it? What put him off the company of other men? What made him prefer hanging round women?

Yet he was like a stranger outside playschool. His were brief excursions into the world of women and, of late, they had been paid for. The women showed him plainly he was no honorary member. He was still Other and the battle lines were drawn. What was the centre of the female world? Dave was at home in it whether it was the furled wetness of a ready cunt or just chatting over tea, when women opened up confidences, their unstitched wounds. He knew the kinds of things women said together, he could imagine those. Men frightened him because his imagination ground to a halt with them.

He took a cloth, soaked in the tang of white spirit, and thoughtfully dabbed off the paint spots on his arms. Paint splattered in the wrong place looks so alarming, so permanent.

Spending so much time at home made Dave competent there. At home he could deal with things. Actually, he should have his own mid-morning TV show, telling others how to do their houses up, keep things looking nice. He thought if he could only bring the world into his own domestic space, then that would make it safe.

Oh, right, he thought, dipping his brush. Safe. Yeah.

One wall left to strip, two to paint, one was complete and pink. Already it was dark outside, a smoky blue night. He'd have to go fetch Laura soon. What had he been thinking of? He didn't even know the bleached mum's name. Hang on – Joanne. He knew the way back to her door by remembering his own steps away: no address. This impersonality shocked him. To think, only hours before he'd shot his load there, left his daughter there and if there was an accident he wouldn't

87

be able to say where he'd been. Somewhere out across this estate, a stranger was sitting with his bairn.

He recalled Laura at about two, speech welling up in her, giving names to her favourite things about her.

Trish she called 'Mimi', which Dave had thought was sweet, but Trish didn't like much. 'Makes me sound like a stripper. Get her to stop.'

His hands were gloved in slick pink. He smeared it on empty patches of wall, leaving prints that looked as if someone had slipped down. The carpet was a right mess. Shit! Pink on blue carpet; they'd been after a boy. He hadn't cleared the squirls of old torn paper before painting, and now they were trodden to mush everywhere. Laura's bed, her belongings, her toys were huddled in the centre. It looked as if there was going to be a jumble sale.

The paint was old, tainted with the tin's rust, and the colour came out patchy. The obstinate shreds of wallpaper he'd left were showing through. It was all a disaster.

Bon Jovi had been playing the whole time on the little cassette player on the floor in the hall.

Could he rely on the woman with the seaside rock wingtip hairdo? Would she think for herself and bring his daughter back to him? Would she think to spare him the trip out?

Dave had decided already, some time ago, he was the type to whom nothing was spared. His was the life all the hard knocks got to. If he was coming downstairs with armfuls of laundry piled above his head, he would be sure to slip down the stairs on dropped socks. He would be the one banging his elbows on hard doorframes.

And look, he couldn't even paint straight. The room echoed dully about him. It was all pink now, wet and streaked in patches. With the dark coming in from the uncurtained window the room looked desolate.

In the past few weeks of his exciting new, secret career move, Dave had seen so many bedrooms. And, in the dark tonight, peering out of the window with no curtains or nets to obstruct him, he thought all the gaps between houses seemed futile. Oughtn't we to pool intimacies more? Shouldn't all these identical little box houses be interconnecting? If they did, Laura wouldn't seem lost to him now, stuck in someone else's world, half an estate away.

Down in the dark street, here was the bleached mum now, bringing his daughter. They were clanging the gate, chatting pleasantly. And up the street came the other mums, like a calm procession, streaming up the tarmac paths, over the scrubby grass. All the mums from outside playgroup with their stained pushchairs and their musical silk roses on their bedside tables and their electric blankets. Each of them coming to his door. Some of them looked up to the lighted window where he stood with his paint roller. An ideal husband.

'Here I am, ladies,' he yelled. He'd already opened the window for the fumes.

'What do *I* think a Cyberman is?'

Trish had poured herself some coffee from the pot Andrew always kept standing ready. He said it was his only vice. He couldn't drink any when he was wrapped up and he tried not to look envious as she took a first sip.

She looked at him fondly. This was their quiet half-hour while he stewed and glinted in his pharaoh's shroud.

'To me a Cyberman is a friendly thing. Not like they used to be when we were kids, when they went shooting people on *Doctor Who*, smacking people on the head and that. Coming out of tombs.

'A Cyberman is a perfect man. His suit is silver and gold, he bristles with light, that curious liquid light that proper jewellery takes on. My Cyberman looks bloody expensive. I am proud to be seen with him.

'He's been custom-built and to the highest standards. Everything they say on adverts about posh cars they could say about him. They could film him running easily, easily, easily, beside a burning field of corn at sunset, playing an Eric Clapton song over the top.

'He has a square jaw, like an old-fashioned hero. His eyes are narrow dark slits. He is suspicious because he is world-wise and because of this he is inured to the world. Sex with him is the safest in the world. He is laminated; his whole body is sheathed.

'Nothing can put my Cyberman off his stroke. Programmed to please, he will let nothing get in the way of his pleasing me. He knows what I expect from my man.

'But he is not a robot, forged to my will. Part of him – a good part – is fleshly still. His electronic body he wears as a shell, an exoskeleton. The underside is sensitive and sheltered. Like a lobster. If I crushed him from behind in a hug, his pliable insides would squirm and ooze through. I love the contrast between the bits of him that are tender and those that are indestructible. Only I know which are which. I see the chinks in his armour. He shows them to me, almost proudly. I can appreciate the way he's had to cobble himself together.'

She smiled at Andy.

'That's what I mean by my Cyberman.'

'Oh.' He smiled unsurely. 'Help me out of all this shit, would you?'

ANEMONES, MY LABRADOR,
HIS PUPPY

WE ALL LIVED, working on our separate, idle little projects, in a slate-grey town that had a history rank with witch burnings and a one-way system of irate traffic as futilely intricate as the patterns inside your ear.

It rained all the time and especially during that last third of the year when they held there, in our nascent Cultural Studies Department, a ten-week course of papers on witches. Papers were given by a variety of visitors in a duskily lit common room which always looked to me like an airport lounge, although I've never flown. An hour of turgid historicism at teatime, Wednesdays; letting somebody's god-awful academic prose wash heedlessly over you, an hour of questions, drinks, then a meal in town, in the same, cramped, crimson room hung with horse brasses and a single, long table, reserved for a set who disturbed other diners with raucous, entirely theoretical talk of sadomasochism, incest, female circumcision.

Julian was beginning his MA on father/son incest in Renaissance drama. He sat at one end of the table, his first night at one of these dos, in a home-made linen shirt, cuffs trailing heartbreakingly in his silver platter of garlic mushrooms. The regulation glossy dark hair flopped over this face arrogant with its own half-apprehension of its beauty; lips quite pink and curling now, with a clumsy wit, as he tried to winkle something noticeable into the conversation between his supervisor, Stephen, and the visiting academic, Ivy.

When Julian laughed it was to draw attention to the post-vocalic 'r' completing each 'ha'; he was making a feature of a rather cultured dippiness. He was all flannels and affected stammer, groping towards the correct critic's name, a distracted hand through hair stylishly awry with three days' grease.

'Yes, my shirt was made for me by my wife,' he told me when I'd said he had oil up the cuffs but that it was a nice shirt anyway. He added, 'She makes all of our clothes; mine and my son's.'

I was making a point of smoking particularly heavily at the meal's end, and working through the last cafetiere, defying the puritanical looks I was getting; the modern critic does not abuse his own body. And I pictured Julian and a whole family togged up in clothes too large for them; the thin and young family, cultured and enunciating properly. Dressing up as grown-ups.

Ivy was the American visiting professor; researching the length and breadth of Britain on instruments of torture used to quieten women. Asked her area of expertise, she would square up her padded shoulders, toss an immaculate Golden Girl perm and declare 'Scolds.' She talked and talked that evening and took a group of us for coffee to the house she had borrowed for a month by the castle.

It was the oldest house I had ever been in, I think, and oddly proportioned; I felt it creak about me as she showed us to a darling little sitting room, and proceeded to slosh coffee onto a milky-coloured carpet. Stephen leaped up to stamp out the stain with J-cloths; all a-sweat now (whereas, minutes earlier, he had been replete with a good meal's strain and an evening of intellectual chitchat). The old house by the castle belonged to a dear friend of his; he was the agent of its rental and blame for the carpet was something he could see reverting straight to him as the patch widened, darkened, and Ivy flapped about, helpless, pissed, and Julian and I sank deep into a plum sofa and chatted, making up a friendship from bits of shared bibliographies and very coy eye contacts.

All this while, past midnight, fog came up over, around the squat castle from the marshes. Ivy hadn't closed her chintz curtains; we were high over the town, quite comfortable, with no need to hide from aggressive passers-by. So the night punched its opacity into the room and I watched Julian's profile; as the Renaissance people chatted, occasionally jotting down names, references, on the backs of their hands.

So this was networking. I could feel Julian thrill with the thought of that beside me on the sofa. On nights like these are important contacts made. Before he had to leave – earlier than the rest of us, for his family – Ivy was dropping big hints his way; interest in his as yet unbegun work, for an anthology she was preparing in Texas on Shakespeare's abusive fathers.

I am not a Renaissance person, but I've read all sorts of things. We came into the early hours talking about the Sitwells. Ivy staggered off to fetch a copy of her last book from her still packed luggage, to show me the cover painting. A young Edith as a captivatingly scarlet woman beside her father.

Stephen began to make noises that it was time to leave. Already Ivy had dropped off once or twice, but she was narcoleptic and we'd been sure – as she'd exhorted us earlier, over coffee – not to mistake her lapses for heavy-handed hints. Still, Stephen felt we oughtn't overstay.

On the pavement outside, beneath the castle still full of condemned men, Ivy told us about the new season at Stratford. Stephen pointed out a hotel's single yellow light; told us that in that very room Dickens and Wilkie Collins had written a ghost story together; some fevered, fond collaboration, on just such a night.

It took some doing to shut Ivy up, get her back indoors and the door locked, to get ourselves free. Stephen was still of a mind to be gentle with her; not so when she returned to Texas a month later, having let the shower run a full week in the empty, ancient house, while she trotted about Scotland peering at gravestones. The house was wrecked.

It was that kind of term; friendships struck up, spectacular as the last fag I lit for my long walk home across town, and damped suddenly down; all trust and bravado lost.

It was a cloying mist that night, coming through bone cold, blue. I said to Stephen, before he turned off towards his swish little place down on the quay, that I thought Julian was very pretty.

The following Sunday evening we were drinking gin in Stephen's flat, shouting between rooms as he braised various things for dinner – I could hear the carrots screaming and spitting in a dish of boiling honey – and I was reading Susan Sontag by his french windows, way above the river.

Once I called him out to watch a woman sitting on a bench by the river, spiting the cold and taking off her socks and shoes very methodically, putting them in her shopping bag. I had to smoke out on the balcony; the flat's distinctly minimalist lines were also supremely health-conscious ones. I took an ashtray decorated with scribbles by Cocteau outside and so missed the young family's arrival. Julian came in with heaps of brightly coloured bedding; cheerful and scarlet he deposited his son on Stephen's bed for the evening and ushered me in so he could explain to us all that they had spent the day walking, out in the hills.

His wife was even younger; some four years younger than me, she was called Elsa and was small, brown, beaming. Yes, she added, they'd been to their church in the country, had lunch with the vicar, and went for a good hard walk afterwards.

Elsa wrote novels; managing three each year, even though she was a full-time mother and wife. We boys looked shamefaced over our starters. She explained that she handwrote several drafts in neat exercise books. Her works were often auto-biographical. Playfully Stephen muttered something about intentionality, textuality; at least something ending in -ality, as most comments *did* in those heady months of high theory and its intrigues.

I helped dish up dessert. 'I think Elsa's a decadent, really,' Stephen hissed. 'Don't be put off by all the talk of church.'

'They're whiter than white!'

'She's a decadent eager to burst out; just listen to her!'

'What does that mean?'

He'd made a kind of plum pudding thing; cloying and spiced.

'I think she's just dying for our Julian to have a man on the side. I think she finds it quite an exciting idea.'

'Oh, right. Yeah.'

I picked up dishes to carry, desultorily. But I was piqued.

When I was doing literary theory research, as I was then, I could never quite get into it. My work was on my contemporaries; other theorists and what they say about other theorists. I was writing about the Subject; subjectivity's awful wrangle with itself in the context of postmodernity. I would treat the library as a shopping mall; I took a trolley now and then between its shelves and my cavalier research consisted of grabbing books whose covers, titles, reputations preceded them or made me fancy them on the spot. My work was chancy and promiscuous and I spent my time picking up choice cuts of quotation; various notable names writing on the subject of the subject, of the body, of identity; all jeopardised now, all their integrity gone. An exciting time to be writing about such things, as my colleagues – their work more absorbing, hierarchised, historical – commented to me. I often worked at home. Sat on the 1940s settee in a rented house by the canal. There I was shanghaied into watching morning television, smoking too many cigarettes.

I bumped into Julian in the corridor and he invited me to dinner, suggesting also that I might like to work with him, in our department, in the small room kept quiet for postgraduates, to be company in these darkening afternoons on the slope down to Christmas. Because of course, one could go mad reading tersely academic discourse in complete solitude. Couldn't we hold each other's hands?

He did a full day, nine to five, since he couldn't work at home, where the Child absorbed hours and love like a doughnut dunked in half-finished coffee. The Postgraduate Room was soundproofed with polystyrene and so he played Stravinsky on an old school-type record player. There was a combination lock on the door; from the jabbing noises made from outside you knew of someone's arrival well in advance. Sometimes we talked about having oak panelling, a fireplace, smart prints; living our most excessive Brideshead fantasies. Those were the fantasies welling head to head across the desk in the middle of the room as we flipped through books, scribbling notes, glancing up now and then. We could relish the indulgences of the other, play opera and flounce about, so long as we kept our heads down at work; him on incest, myself on transvestism as a metaphor for postmodern subjectivity.

He took to wearing full linen suits, stripey sailor tops and I – God help me – knotted my paisley scarves as the weather took a colder turn and I bought a long dark coat.

Our department was in a building cobbled together in 1966 but it had a grassy quad crisscrossed by paving stones and here we could meet in the lowering gloom and hold conversations about nothing, before saying ta-ra till tomorrow morning.

Well, if not nothing, at least about homoeroticism in *Henry V*. Remember: 'A little touch of Harry in the night?' Harry's erotic largesse, dispensing himself, his body, about the sleeping troops the night before battle. Oh, that was the kind of thing to be made a meal of, here in Cult Stud. We were Cult Studs all right. I lent him my video of *My Own Private Idaho*; he was extremely keen on the homoerotic motif. It was the mortar which held Western culture's tenets in place; even in a fractured modernity. Rome was built solely from men rubbing each other up the wrong way. He evinced a keen, theoretical interest; steam blowing out over his coat collar as we stood in the quad. Gave me a kind of mock punch before running off to fetch the Child from the crèche. He carried a daft little suitcase about with him. Once, giving me a lift back one frozen night, he went to a car that looked only a little like his and, mistaking it, tried to force the lock. For hapless things like these I can feel a quirk of fondness; other times ineptness in someone with whom I've had odd, difficult scenes just makes me impatient and sick.

*　　*　　*

96

Another American woman! At the meal with Julian and Elsa. She was another writer, who lived near Washington in an entirely green farmhouse with a mother who thought she was Miss Lavish from *A Room with a View* and who, upon reading one of my letters to her daughter, Teri, had declared: 'He is one of us.' Things had looked promising for me and Teri, then; almost coaxed into a full-time heterosexuality by the promise of being one of the people who live in a green house in Washington and who *understand each other*. At weak moments the promise of being understood is enough to tempt me to anything.

So we'd fucked and had a few nice talks, meals, awkward scenes. The marrieds invited us to coo over their house in the terrace by the park. A piano of blond wood dominated their dining room. There were shelves of bright new hardbacks; Elsa talked of A.S. Byatt, Alan Hollinghurst, how she loved gay fiction and thought she might really adore being a gay man. The Child woke once upstairs as wine was mulling on the open fire and was brought down in a blanket, fierce, warm as cheese on toast, to be inspected. My heart went out, as it always does, to kids, babies, anyone without an ounce of guile.

I sat across from Teri. She was chewing on fat and bones; we ate pheasant, plucked fresh from the market. Her eyes wide with disgust at its gaminess. 'It was,' she told me the following week, 'the worst thing I have tasted in all my life.' To me it looked a little raw; those pink, streaming ends of bones. But what did I know? At least one and a half class distinctions away from an understanding of poultry, our birds were always banged in the slammer for four hours a time; we were terrified of salmonella. With knowledge and class comes an insouciant carelessness. That night we sucked slivers of steamed courgette dipped in sour cream and Teri had fallen quiet, grimacing.

I stood in the road with Julian, right up on the hill above the town. A fag outside since they, too, were conscious of health. We looked at the real smoke coming from his chimney; that inscrutable, solid blue. 'Signifying everything I protect,' he said, with a rare flash of earnestness. The arc lamps of the cathedral distorted the plumes' shapes weirdly; they made an umbrella. He gave me his scarf and leather driving gloves since it had begun to snow and I had a fair way to walk home. And he told me he never drank much because of his mother's problems with it. His father owned a company in America and lived there now. I heard Julian phone him for free from the room where we worked. He often phoned his wife, too, while she wrote her novels in exercise books at home. And they talked baby talk for minutes on end. The first time I heard it I went scarlet; a problem I never had with eavesdropping usually. Hearing him babytalk was worse than nudging his foot under the desk with my own, accidentally, as we worked; breaking the braced weight of our tension clean across and patching it with an embarrassed smile. We watched the smoke go up a bit longer and then I had to get home. We didn't hug good night; we never did. I walked down the middle of the road, as advised, to the bottom of the hill.

We had a friendship developing which wasn't bluff, hearty, cruel, as two straight men might seem to us. It wasn't implicit with use and suspicion like two openly gay men. We were romantic friends.

'We have a very romantic friendship,' he told me on the phone the following teatime. He'd rung to say Teri was about to become engaged to some Irish bloke and get her dual citizenship.

'We do?' I was sitting on the top stair at home.

'You're a very romantic figure in our department,' he said. 'Rupert Brooke.'

'Fucking great.' Then I delivered a short lecture on flirtatiousness. How I thought people ought to take responsibility for the signals they give off. Watch how you signify; it's all a language. He thanked me, a little warily. 'You're a wise man!' was how he ended the phone call; hearty, bluff, casual. I put the phone down wondering why I'd lectured him on messing about with things he couldn't carry through. It was a warning

98

in advance, I thought; just in case he got ideas. Bless him; had he an idea in his head? Oh, it was all high theory and his work seemed prohibitively complex, but he had as much sense as a Labrador I'd kept when I was seven who'd been called, incidentally, Julian. The same brown lucidity in his eyes; a careless and distracted fidelity.

To take my mind off research which had a disturbing knack of creeping up on me every minute of the day and waking me at night with its implications, its references, its myriad, swimming footnotes, I had taken up drawing again. I filled a thick sketchpad each month with scratchy sub-Hockney line drawings. Rooms quivering with poignancy and cluttered everyday use, figures observed from afar in the very act of the humdrum and, more recently, figures and faces of those about me. My fascination with getting their expressions down for all time as if they might suddenly be lost to me in their most ordinary, usual aspects, is apparent now, when I flick through the books, in the way each drawing is labelled and dated. My sketchpads of the time have their own indexed, academic coherence; as if I'd set about cataloguing my friends. I was alert; an old hand at having friends in a town where people do research and come to talk about books; they pass you by. It's a relay race and the baton is something you can't afford not to fling away from you, heartlessly, when need be.

I needed to draw, to have days off, to do things other than read and write in the locked Postgraduate Room. Its windows steamed up with claustrophobia, it seemed. The white board was smeared with words as though they flew about the room like Hitchcock's birds when we weren't looking, then flattened themselves to the board when we were. Julian's desperate concentration wore me out, too; sometimes he was too panicked to break up a morning for coffee. When we did have coffee, in a campus bar with red gingham tablecloths, his conversation was weak and repetitive and you could tell he was just worried about his note-taking on the Renaissance. I'd forgotten, in a year, how intensive MAs can be. I was out to pasture in the grassless hinterlands of a PhD.

So I relished my days at home; breakfast watching the frozen canal and its swans turned clumsy, skidding their way about. The canal went dusty with layers of snow; it was like *Orlando*. I had the cat twisting about beside me, and I drew some anemones we had on the mantelpiece until half nine that morning, until Julian arrived, fresh from dropping the Child at the crèche. I'd persuaded Julian he needed the odd day away from our soundproofed room, too, and, given the circumstances we'd settled on, he agreed.

'Ready?' he asked breezily when I opened the front door. He had his flat cap on, jauntily; wrapped up for winter. He looked determined and businesslike, as he always did when going for piles of research texts in the library. Today's activity was something he was equally set on doing right. Meanwhile I was quivering inwardly, having expected him to have run a mile by now, all resolution, curiosity gone. While I made us a pot of tea I found I couldn't swallow and just nodded as he fussed about with conversation.

'I ehm . . .' he stumbled, and I passed him his tea. He struggled to take off his coat and hat, still holding it. Perhaps he'd gone as nervous as I by now. 'I told Elsa about this. Asked her, really, if she thought it was all right.'

I took a scalding sip of Earl Grey. Earl Grey was something else we concurred on alongside Michael Nyman's music, Chagall's circus paintings. 'And?'

'She didn't see why I even mentioned it. She says it's up to us. But she'd like to see what we come up with. If you don't mind . . .'

I shrugged.

A week ago there'd been a coffee break over scarlet gingham. We'd been joined by Teri and Elsa and Teri's talk of marriage. She wanted to piss me off, did so, and left. Elsa went after her, a little later; they were doing a writing course together.

Left alone again, Julian started asking me about my drawing. He showed me some contact prints of his he'd done in a rented darkroom the previous night. He had whole films of statues from Italy. Pearly white men stretched out and, in these mismatched, tiny contacts, interlocking in a bizarre panoply. Then there was a film of Stephen, dressed in his usual crumpled cords and jacket, in a dusty room, lying, standing or sitting in a glass cabinet. Julian explained that these were all his father figures; their poses paralleling one another. Oh boy. I said I thought they were very nice and that I'd like to see them finished.

'And,' I added, pouring more tea, 'if you ever have film left over, I'd love some nice, proper photos taken of me. I've never had any done, really.'

'Of course, of course,' he said in that rushed, cajoling tone, one eye on the clock and the other on the next topic of interest, as though wary of being caught out.

We talked about Roland Barthes or something or other for a bit, before Julian said, 'Of course, what I'd like to do is photograph a bloke naked. That's what I really need.'

I coloured again but couldn't let the conversation drop. 'I don't know about that . . .'

'Oh! I wasn't asking you . . . I just meant . . .' He floundered and my heart went out to him again, as it was tending to do. 'Would you, though?'

I felt I had a dire body and, in my excited indecision, felt it sliding, like molten butter, into slabs about my feet.

'We'd draw up a bargain,' I said.

'What for?'

'I've got the same problem drawing. The next thing I need is a nude model, and I want a man. But who do you ask? How can you ask?'

We giggled in complicity.

'But we understand each other . . . where we're at . . . and our romantic friendship. It needn't be a problem. Why don't we pose for each other? Make it mutual?'

'A mutual appreciation society.' He smiled.

Held every Wednesday and Friday morning, we decided. And I would put the central heating on full blast, pull down the blinds in my tiny bedroom, switch on the lamps, get the

101

Nyman CDs ready. We needed an atmosphere redolent with trust and artifice to see us through.

Into this warmth and conspiracy, Julian actually turned up that first Wednesday morning. He walked into my room ahead of me as we came up carrying our cups of tea. He wore the expression of a potential house buyer and looked down at my drawing book and pens, pencils slung as if nonchalantly on the bed. He turned to smile at this and carefully put his posh camera to one side. I switched the music on and sat on a chair, finding I couldn't actually say anything now we were here.

He produced a very old hardback. 'I'm afraid I'm sticking to the other condition. That I'm allowed to read while you draw, since it could go on some time.'

'Fine,' I nodded, and he tossed it onto my duvet and then shrugged his heavy jumper off over his head, fluffing up his hair as he emerged. His home-made shirt was rucked up; he tugged it and revealed a sparrow-thin torso which goose-fleshed over at first, its delicate nipples startled, on end. He was braced like a bird's skeleton on the bed as he prepared to pose; milk-bottle white, fragile, a mass of shifting, fluent shades of cream and blue-grey. I judged and altered trapezoids, rhombuses of bones and shallow muscle and he carried his old book through all of these negotiations, keeping his eyes on the small print. He wrenched off shoes and socks, slinging them, followed by his trousers. Suddenly, he stood beside my bed in cotton undershorts and I had a moment of ontological doubt how he could be revealed so beautifully explicit to me by means other than an idealising imagination or the fervid mutual decision that we were about to fuck. Yet it was neither of these things and terribly, frustratingly realistic as he took down his pants and sprawled almost hairless and wan across the bed, the thick hooded nub of his cock slapping against his stomach and lolling under my nose.

There were so very few poses, it turned out. Sprawling contextless provides the average body with a limited amount of things to do. I interrupted his reading each quarter hour for something new.

He flipped about. 'It's cock or arsehole,' he said, showing a streak of vulgarity I'd not heard before and more shocking, strangely, than his actions of that moment; belly down on the now-rumpled bed, raising his arse to display his pendulous prick, neat little balls.

My part of the bargain was to be naked too as I drew him; ready for the photos he wanted to take in the bathroom. We lay side by side and I scratched away at the page; each drawing had its lavish crest of pubic hair and his prick looking different each time. It seemed natural to both of us that what we really wanted represented was his face, his cock, the smooth chest and stomach between. When he looked at the progress made he was fascinated by what I'd made of his cock. 'It looks like a little face!' he said.

I undressed fearing that I'd get an erection, but I figured that, that being inevitable for both of us, we'd deal with it all right. I didn't, however; hung limp and small alongside him. Julian appeared to cast the most cursory of glances.

But I stood against our half-plastered, dramatic bathroom walls and he closed in on my skin, the shadings of muscle, the sullen defiance of my cock and murmured lovingly at it all through his viewfinder. He shot his pictures still naked and when he leaned in to show me how things focused, how light was squeezed out, nonchalantly brought us into contact and I felt my dick slide wetly along his thigh with a trail of precum.

When I flipped through the drawings for Elsa over our next meal together – at my house this time – I noticed a shocking continuity for the first time. She had expressly asked to see them and, embarrassed, Julian and I said she could. She picked up on this certain feature immediately. Julian's cock was bigger, more alert in each drawing. By the last, warmest, most faithful version, he was sprawled entirely safe and sleepy and drawn from waist level. So safe and guileless he lay, giving a thoughtlessly rude view of a vulnerable, puckered arsehole and his thick cock arched up his belly as if to drink from the well of his navel. It hadn't struck me before but in this drawing his foreskin was drawn back of its own accord, to reveal a tender, blushing dome; the urethra's needle eye. He had a negligent, luxurious erection. The pose was so calm and accustomed, I hadn't noticed. And how do you test hardness, readiness, with the circumspection we basked in?

At the front of the Halifax there was one of those little tables for the kiddies, cluttered with Lego. The Child and I played there while Julian queued up, cap literally in hand, for the counter. We were making a tower sort of thing, putting a kind of conversation together. The Child was stuffed into a blue and yellow romper suit; when we walked through town Julian slung him carelessly arm to arm and it was as if the Child bounced, resilient, squalling, and attracting the attention of each shopkeeper we met.

Especially in the indoor market they were known and watched out for; primped and petted, the young father and son exhibiting this astonishing precocity at buying their own groceries. Friday afternoons were when Julian had the Child to himself. This one in November was my birthday and we were having lunch together; at a table strewn with red, white and blue napkins in Café Monet.

We spent all afternoon round town and it was dark before the shops shut. We were a family. A gay couple and child. And we basked in the fondness of shopkeepers. How nice it was for them to see how we were coming on. Nice to see the young ones managing. We were laden down with shopping. We bought Earl Grey in a speciality shop where everything came in redolent wooden kegs and barrels. I was learning that Julian and family liked to buy things which were, if not expensive, at least authentic. Handwrapped parcels of moist, fresh, loose tea, authentically dead and dripping birds hung outside butchers' windows. I got caught up in it and it made me feel more bogus than ever; me with my penchant for snooping round Just What You Need and Superdrug.

That night, the night of my twenty-fourth, I had a lovely time with a friend of mine in a cocktail bar done up exactly like the studio set for *The Scarlet Empress*. My friend was a sternly phlegmatic, one-handed fencing instructor. He took me to task.

'You're fucking with the bourgeoisie,' he warned, adjusting his glasses and sucking on his cocktail straw. He'd recently done a counselling course and, while he kept the tone of voice they'd given him, he threw out their ideas of objectivity. 'Or rather, the bourgeoisie are fucking you. They always do. You never win. Don't bother with it. Don't be daft.'

I frowned, sunk into myself. 'It's just a laugh. I need a laugh. There's no risk. Nothing's happened. I can lap up a morning or two of mutual glorification with no strings attached and not get hurt.'

'I dunno,' he said. I wasn't sure if that cast doubt on me or the situation. He added, 'It's a complex one. Because you reckon that he's really a queer, don't you?'

'Oh, God, I can't tell anything any more.'

Nowadays I just thought all sex was pretty androgynous. This caused problems for me in Cult Stud where centuries' worth of accumulated theoretical discourse told me that there were all sorts of differences to be problematised.

Yet . . . regardless of the biological accoutrements of the bodies I had encountered, their lovemaking always occurred to me as an androgynous affair. Sleek, lightly haired limbs folded about one another or reserved in a charged proximity. Their very vulnerability in the act or the presence of love helped them transcend gender. Surely.

'Bollocks,' said my fencing friend. 'You're queer or you're straight and anything else is just fucking around. Tell him to get himself sorted.'

We wandered home that night and he got me to promise to stop fucking about. He took the radical position. It wasn't fair to expect people – me, since he was being supportive here – to stand in the background, in their own marginal position and let others – straights, he spat – get away without commitment.

'Bourgeois fucking straights,' he sneered as we walked

105

along the slimy towpath. We went to mine for coffee, and
watched Ken Russell's *Women in Love* off video.

On the mantelpiece – and the fencer commented on them
– in my gorgeous blue Habitat vase: a squashed bouquet
of shocking pink and midnight anemones. Their stalks bent
beneath the dull black weight of their hearts, and their vellum
petals sodden and bruised.

Walking back at teatime, Julian had made me wait outside
Interflora with the Child. I had a feeling what he was up to.
A nice gesture. A kiss-off. A promise. The Child flapped his
arms to be picked up as it came on to freezing rain and I
did so and received for my pains a swift, grateful hug. Julian
came out with his shoulders hunched, brandishing his prize.
He had two separate parcels of dark, glamorous flowers.

'One for Mummy and one . . .' he gave me mine, 'for
you.'

THE LION VANISHES

I WAS HEAVILY involved reading something and I never noticed when we stopped. When I'm on a train I like to keep my head down much of the time. It doesn't do to have people think you're looking at them. Anything might result.

It was a busy train, a trans-Europe express – of Agatha Christie and Kraftwerk fame – and we were crammed into compartments that reeked of pine, tobacco and musty plush. The woman sitting across from me was clutching three sticky cases of Belgian chocolates, a leopard-skin pillbox hat resting ominously on the shelf above her head. Up to no good, I thought, and went to the dining compartment for lunch, not wanting to be involved.

At this stage our journey was all mountains and forests. I hardly knew where we were; if not hurtling through invisible, snowstormed countryside, we alternated wildly between the dizzying clarity of the severest of altitudes and the vegetable dark of the woods. The landscape was something else, besides my fellow travellers, not to get too embroiled in.

I review books, novels. I had a suitcase of twenty-six in the luggage carriage and by Manchester, England, was meant to have read and commented on each. I was on number twelve, a heady and baroquely inaccurate account of the execution of Mary Queen of Scots and was anticipating another quiet afternoon in a semi-doze with somebody else's fiction at my mercy, flipping the pages with a disrespectful haste.

The quiet of the train was fascinating. A quiet tamped down by all the snow, which we could see but, since we were kept in this Regency-stripe-flocked shuttle, not even imagine tasting or touching. The climate's unaffected quiet infected everyone, I thought.

I had developed my sea legs, train legs, and I was buffeted all the way to the dining car, which was only two up from the last, the luggage car. I was very familiar with this last, since with each hardback book completed, I had to make another trip to replace it from my case. It was awkward, but I didn't like to carry piles of books around with me the whole journey, drawing attention to myself.

In the luggage car, also, in that workmanlike place full of yellow dust and shunting boxes and cases and crates, were the magician's stage props. I'd known we had a magician on board; I'd seen him clearing tablecloths for applause at dinnertime.

He was the shape of a purple pear and fit to burst through his immaculate evening dress, which he wore all day with a ludicrous top hat. He had a malevolent waxed moustache; as if he should stop the train and tie us all to the rails. He impressed everyone and we clapped at his antics with the crockery. After three days it palled and now he was quiet and not as showy. It doesn't do to become too well known on a long trip, to be a prominent personality. We know that from disaster movies, don't we? The mouthy characters (played by someone famous, known for doing quirky types) are the ones who'll be killed, heroically perhaps, but pathetically and quite definitely. Think of Shelley Winters in *The Poseidon Adventure*.

So our magician kept his trap shut and soon we'd almost forgotten about him and his tricks. As the days in the interminable mountains slid by, he became dowdier and dowdier. There he was, this evening, sucking soup from a dull gold spoon in a shady corner of the dining car. His glasses were opaque and his shoulders hunched. I worried for him, even, that he mightn't pluck up his charisma before arriving in Germany, where he was to start performing again. His assistant, Deborah, had shed her sequins and feathers and, sitting opposite him with a meagre salad, looked like an old man's secretary.

When I went to swap my book I would spend a surreptitious hour among the luggage and stage props of the magician and his assistant. God forbid that anyone should have found me in those joyful hours. In her spangly outfits with a feather boa slung I'd be lying inside her glittering coffin and waiting to be sawed into two or three with his doves and rabbits and what have you nibbling and scampering and shedding bits of themselves all around me. I've always fancied myself as someone's assistant. Preferably in show business.

But this far into the trip I'd grown cocky, I'm afraid. I look back upon my nonchalance – delaying lunch, breezing through the dining room with the feigned intention of changing my book first – with a judder of self-loathing. But there I go, blithely telling André the waiter to wait half an hour before bringing my starter and sashaying past the magician's table where his cutlery is attached to the table by slender golden chains, though it needn't be, with him being magical and all.

I flung open his cabinet and breathed short ecstatic breaths on its lacquered surfaces. I felt right into the corners of his mysterious carpetbags with a trembling hand: what new stuff could I find? The doves cooed and nudged each other, watching me stripping quickly and donning her shimmering stage underwear. An alpine-pure bunny scampered to the top of a pile of boxes to quiz my urgent erection as I lay down with a sigh in the sawing cabinet. To the rabbit it was a newcomer which might upstage him in the act. I concentrated on the exhibition I made for myself and only me. In this last carriage of the train we rocked and creaked with the awesome menace of the deep winter woods. Time slipped away from me, as it always does when I'm messing about.

And then – oh, God – like a terrible moment in an old, old melodrama, there's the magician's waxed moustache twitching in furious indignation above me. His eyes bulge and I expect a card, stencilled in white letters, to appear between us:

You cheeky bastard! What the fuck are you up to?

But it doesn't come. The magician, it turns out, really is

Italian, knows no English and, anyway, finds my hideously exposed recumbence and masturbatory fantasy life uproariously funny. Entirely at his mercy I submit to his terrifying giggles and then, wiping tears and turning to go with a stream of what for all I know could be evil oaths and threats, he bends and kisses me hard, thrusting a massive, palpitating tongue into my mouth. Then he's gone.

I die of embarrassment.

The very worst thing about resuming my place in the restaurant car and trying to eat lunch with a measure of equanimity was knowing that the magician would be sitting at his table, only yards away, telling Deborah all about me, his mouth still wet with that stolen kiss.

I had much rather eat my lunch in however intolerable a situation than fling myself off the train, so I swallowed my pride and went back to my place, determined to ignore them.

Two things had changed and they saved my face.

Deborah had gone from their table. The magician ignored me as I went by with my book and he'd gone back to being nondescript. The second change didn't hit me until after André had brought my soup and I was well into the first chapter of the Queen of Scots schlock-horror. The train had stopped; we were completely stationary in the suddenly distinct and terrifying woods and at last sound was beginning to creep in from outside. We had arrived – but in the middle of nowhere.

Very slowly I closed my book.

I looked out of the window. The forest had a majesty and horrible glamour you quite missed while hurtling through it on a train. It looked very much like some queer gigantic beast's larder. These weren't trees and clearings designed for the aesthetic sense and sensibilities of Western human beings. Everything we relish is deciduous. Nothing, I was sure, grew naturally, fruitily and juicily in this place. The woods were an aggregate of slate and ice and their vegetation was undoubtedly nine tenths poison. Some of my fellow travellers

110

had started to talk, in whispers. They still sounded aggrieved and *safe*. I was already discomforted by the magician's kiss: I knew we were up to our necks in it.

Into our poised silence came Deborah, with that breezy glamour of her own. She went straight to the magician.

'Miss Farquar has vanished,' she hissed. Heads turned.

'Who?' he asked, as if looking past her at somebody else.

'Miss Farquar! The elderly lady we met at dinner a couple of nights ago. An eccentric old lady in a leopard-skin pillbox hat you said had the look of a smuggler about her.'

'Did I?' the magician purred and I realised they were talking English.

'She's just gone! Flown the coop! How can she just vanish off a moving train?'

'We've stopped now, my dear.' An indolence in his voice; he indulges her and likes to draw attention to himself. Which he is doing, as cutlery is put down with little clinks and rattles of golden chains.

'She had vanished well before we stopped! I was looking for her when we did. Anyway . . .' Deborah glances about with a frown. She hates the inefficient. 'Why have we stopped?'

'That's what I'd like to know!' shouts a gruff extra in a brown pinstriped suit.

'Yes!' adds another, an auntyish type, rather haplessly. 'We all have appointments to keep. Why hasn't the captain informed us?'

The magician laughs shortly. 'Trains, as far as I know, do not have captains.'

'They have *some*thing!' the aunty replies curtly. She's carrying some kind of cat. 'And why can't you spirit us back on the right tracks if you're such a wizard at magic?'

He goes on laughing as if he hadn't a care in the world.

'Did anybody else see what happened to Miss Farquar?' Deborah asks, with just a steely hint of desperation in her voice now, which is unusual for someone routinely stabbed and sawn up on stage. 'I'm rather worried about her now; you see, she was elderly and diabetic, she said . . .'

The frowsty aunty said, 'I'm sure I don't know who you mean,' before turning back to her lunch.

'You must have noticed her. She always had a leopard-skin pillbox hat with her. She carried it obsessively as you do your cat, or that man does a recent book. As if she had something precious and rare sewn into its lining.'

The man in the brown suit shrugged and he too returned to his meal, as did the others, all refusing to remember Miss Farquar.

'But you must recall her! She was such a personality!'

And Deborah's eyes hit on me then. I squirmed under that momentary glance. I felt she must see through my waistcoat, see her fake jewel-encrusted basque – which I hadn't had time to remove – beneath.

'You! The journalist – you were in her compartment, weren't you?'

With the faint sound of the cock crowing accusations of betrayal in my popping ears, I shook my head and returned to my book and my soup.

Deborah gave a faintly hysterical grunt of frustration. She called out, 'I'm going to investigate this! It's not me going mad! You're not getting me to think that!'

She stalked off towards the front end of the train, going for official assistance.

The magician called after her, 'While you're about it, my dear, you might as well ask why we've stopped. This is, actually, ridiculous.'

She had left a couple of pink feathers behind her on the dining-car floor. André trod them into the pile when he cleared my table. They must have dropped out from under her travelling clothes when she was stamping her heel in indignation. Did she, too, wear stage clothes underneath her demure outer layers?

Back in my compartment I sat alone, stomach grumbling a habitual dream of indigestion brought on, no doubt, by my reviewee's prose. I started to skim-read, which I only do in the greatest of emergencies. My compartment was otherwise empty; the two nuns and the schoolgirl weren't back yet from wherever they went. They were quite as vanished as the elderly Miss Farquar in her leopard-skin hat.

I might have told Deborah: yes, of course Miss Farquar was and is real. I have spent much of this endless journey avoiding that roving, weeping eye of hers. But why should I do Deborah any favours? Fuck her! She's got exactly the job and the lifestyle I should kill for. Well, not quite. My palate and vocabulary had picked up a faintly gothic air from my recent reading.

And at this point through my carriage window I saw two lions fucking in the undergrowth. Quite extraordinary and unabashed they were at it. Their shaggy, remorseless, leonine copulation. Vivid and auburn against the icing-sugar snow, they tumbled each other and ploughed up little showers of brilliance. Their lolling tongues were a decided hot pink in that frigid clearing.

I watched with a fascination excused only by the uniqueness of this privileged, TV-documentary proximity. They were magnificent and, when I think back, I wonder if I have since invented some of the tender and complicit caresses this king and queen of the forest exchanged. There was a sureness and equality about their performance . . . Did I really see her snag his golden, furry prick and balls and roll them about in her slavering, deadly jaws? Watch him bark in pleasure as she released them, safe, and his cock was shiny and sticky like the fresh bud of a horsechestnut; but immense indeed?

And did he toss back that fabulous dreadlocked mane while she sprawled dangerously before him and then did he lick and lap at her cunt, occasionally tossing spumes of fresh snow her way to tease her and cool her and dabbled at her again with his strong tongue. All around their superbly engined bodies the snow crept its thickness back as if drawing down the sheets, pulling them deeper into bed. In truth, I thought, it was their fierceness with each other that melted all about them and set up an energetic drizzle of dead icicles from the branches above them. They romped and I watched – for how long?

Long enough for the nuns to return to our car.

When the door shot open and they eased their gentle, shrouded selves inside, I jumped as if poked and yanked down the Liberty-print blind. Surely, I thought, still sweating as they nodded and smiled at me in their foreign language, they could hear the silent frolic outside? Orgasm has its own pitch and sounds thunderous to everyone attuned to it, surely? But with the blind down they were oblivious to what was going on outside.

Irritably I pretended to be reading again and we all set about looking impatient for the off. But actually, I wanted to stay for a while and watch the lions' glorious pride in lovemaking. It galled me that I was missing out on this grand, no-holds-barred demonstration of a bestial mutuality. We could all do with such a display, I thought.

It was then, in my crossness, I looked at the floor of the carriage in an effort to prevent myself flinging up the blind once more, and I noticed that both nuns wore under their habits scarlet high heels.

Shit! the cultural critic and journalist that I am thought. Why is that so familiar? What Hitchcock film did nuns wear high heels in?

I set to work thinking hard and fast; blocking out the after-image and afterglow that still had me blushing. Which film was it? This is the kind of thing I'm meant to be up on.

The door opened again and I expected it to be that brat from the Swiss finishing school, but it wasn't; it was Deborah, looking pink and cross. She smiled tersely and let herself in, followed by a black porter and a wryly amused magician. The magician gave me a special smile and I blushed even harder.

'This lady is looking for another lady she says belonged to this compartment,' the porter began. He wore a gorgeous purple suit with gold braid. Portering seemed like quite a good deal if that was the drag that went with it.

'Sorry,' I said, just wanting everyone to leave me alone so I could see if the lions were still out there or not. It also occurred to me that something else might be going on. It had struck me earlier that Miss Farquar with her boxes of sticky Belgian chocolates and her leopard-skin pillbox hat was up to no good. What if this was some kind of intelligence test, or a spying deal and they were testing us out?

Best say nothing. So I clammed up, to the porter's relief, Deborah's pique and the magician's further wry amusement. He followed them out with that wily, magical glint in his eye, tipping his hat to the nuns who, similarly and presumably for reasons of their own, had apparently never clapped eyes on Miss Farquar. He tipped his hat to me too with, if I wasn't mistaken, distinctly salacious intent. The fucker!

Just go, piss off, just go, I was thinking and aiming it at the nuns. They sat there, though, and one took out her knitting. Red high heels! I thought. Well, I never! We all have little foibles.

It started coming back to me. The Hitchcock film was one where the nun obviously isn't what she seems. She's a prostitute or something, and she is looking after a corpse, which is all bandaged beyond recognition and en route to somewhere in Europe and is . . . on a train!

Across the compartment both nuns tapped their red slinky feet to a secret rhythm. They set up an unconscious tattoo mimicking train noises. They wanted to be off, but their faces beamed nothing but contentment.

And it was a train that stopped unexpectedly . . . something to do with spies in wartime. There were fierce SS men stuck out hidden in the undergrowth, shooting at the passengers in the stationary, derailed train. And the tarty nun in the high heels got shot! Near the end of the film. That's right! It was Hitchcock's wartime propaganda movie. That was the one.

And the train had stopped because . . . the spy was on board, swathed in bandages and she'd been found . . . by a young woman looking for . . . an elderly woman she'd befriended en route to England . . . who had vanished inexplicably and now turned out to be a dangerous spy.

It was a fabulous film and you ought to see it.

Since my little adventure I've meant to hire it or buy it, but it's one of those things you just don't get round to. *The*

Lady Vanishes. I'd still like to see how close we came, that afternoon, to being just like the film.

I went to the toilet and stood on its carved wooden seat to look through the slit of a window. I could just – only just – see the rowdy big cats going for it. It was a mammoth session.

A knock at the bathroom door. We'd been pitched into a disaster movie, but were still terribly polite, it seemed. 'Hang on,' I piped, flushing the chain, washing my hands, but the door flew open and the magician stepped in, locking it behind him.

'You might just wait,' I told him crossly, drying my hands.

Eyeing a sash of glittering fabric which I had poking out from under my waistcoat, he sneered.

'Deborah thinks you are lying about the existence of her friend Miss Farquar, in an effort to prove her mad.'

I gave a decent impersonation of a snort of incredulity. 'Why should I want to do that?'

He was squat and heavy and his pointed beard was a glossy black. He was devilish and swift and in a split second upon me, forcing me back against the cistern and thrusting that beard in my face.

'I don't mind if you do drive Deborah mad,' he hissed. 'Wouldn't you like to replace her in my magic box?'

He chuckled greasily and kissed me as before. But when he drew back I surprised him. Kissed him back and thrust my tongue for good measure between his tiny, shiny teeth.

The magician's eyebrows raised together and I could tell he was pleased. He licked his lips, sucked his teeth slowly, as if tasting wine. We tried it again and he released his grip on me, though it became no less ardent.

'Carry on.' He grinned. 'We'll get rid of my present assistant together.'

When I returned to my compartment the nuns were gone. The lino was peppered with depressions from their heels.

I flicked up the blind. The lions were gone.

Or rather, the lion was gone.

116

Sprawled in elegant torpor, exhausted in his heartless absence, the spent but regal lioness occupied pride of place in the ruinous calm of the glade. She was all but smoking a post-coital cigarette. Knocked askance on her beautiful brow – a wonder I hadn't noticed it earlier – was a leopard-skin pillbox hat.

OCARINA

WE WERE AT this party after a poetry reading in Darlington. It was late and we weren't planning to stay for much longer but we sat on the Tuscany patio for a couple more drinks. In the dark we struggled to find places on the wall, moving urns of flowers aside and feeling the concrete for spilled wine. As time got on, the patio started to fill up. It was the most popular spot.

The party was a surprise. One of the poets had flung her home open to all and sundry. Inside and out there were paper lanterns and nibbles. What made it exotic was the number of fish tanks Chelsea kept.

'This evening I have come as a mermaid,' she'd been telling everyone. She was a psychiatric nurse and was stretched into an indigo sheath. When the party was on she slunk about between poets and hangers-on, holding plates aloft and tantalising everyone with snacks. Lucky she's got big hands, I thought. She put me in mind of a transvestite I'd had in a novel I wrote the previous year.

Chelsea's teenage daughters and son had been roped in to pour drinks and serve gateaux. I noticed that after a certain point they had given up to sit on the staircase and pass a bottle of vodka between them, watching the proceedings with bored eyes. All up the tall staircase there were alcoves set into the wall. More fish, swimming.

The patio windows were slid back, gaping, and the whole house was fragrant with a summer night in Darlington. The woman who ran the poetry group – a poet in her own right – sat in a deck chair in the centre of the flagstones and sobbed

118

into her wineglass. She waved her free hand as if ready to
add something pertinent once she had finished crying.

We really had to go soon. There was quite a drive. You were
driving so you only sipped your drink. You read well tonight,
I thought. I wouldn't touch the broccoli quiche. There was
already some folded discreetly into the urn beside me.

Somebody smashed a glass and it sounded musical.

Inside Chelsea's extension, beyond the spread french windows, two soft settees faced each other. Animated conversation, laughing, choking on crisps and bubbles. Pairs of tired
feet tangled and toyed with their shoes and blocked the way
back into the extension. Chelsea was perched on her new
boyfriend's knee, feeding him trifle with her fingers.

He had a green chin and laughed deep in his throat when
she tried to stick a cherry up his nose. He wore a navy blazer
and shiny shoes. His hair was cut short. Looked like he played
sports. Off-duty policeman, I thought. Chelsea ruffled the
stubble on his head.

'Margaret,' you said, smiling in welcome because Margaret
had lurched through the ferns with her paper plate and glass
to talk to us. You cleared a seat for her. She was struggling
with her nibbles and drink and that walking stick.

'I liked your work tonight,' I said.

She looked at me long and hard. At first I thought she had
a suspicious look about her. But she was just thoughtful and
on something for her nerves. Then she smiled.

'It was from my erotic sequence,' she told us. 'I wasn't
sure whether to give it an airing tonight.'

'I think you made the right decision.'

'I think so, too. Did I tell you I've been put into an
anthology of erotica?'

She raised her voice to tell us this. Some of the poets
nearby must have heard. They nudged each other and, in
her deck chair, the poet in her own right briefly stopped
waggling her hand.

'I know I look old now,' Margaret said to me. She had
one of those disconcerting glimmers in her eyes. The young

at heart addressing callow youth and hoping to shock. 'But I've had a surprisingly rich erotic life in my time.'

'Have you now?' I lit a cigarette and noticed you had started talking to Chelsea and her friend. My filter had fuchsia lipstick on it, which surprised me. I thought it would have rubbed off already. I had come dressed as one of Genet's sailors, which seemed quite a flash thing to do in Darlington.

Someone had changed the record, prompting Margaret to say, 'Prokofiev. Listen. Nothing like woodwind to get me going.' She used her cane to bang time on the flagstones.

You and Chelsea and the rugby player were pissing your-selves about something. The poet in the deck chair had gone back to crying.

'Do you know, there's nothing as seductive as a man who can play a clarinet well.'

I said, 'I've got an uncle who plays clarinet. He's a dentist.'

'I fell in love with a clarinet player when he was playing. He seduced me utterly and he wasn't even aware of my presence. My existence, even. I watched him all night. Black hair slicked down with wax so it looked painted on an egg. Serious expression. Lovely evening dress. And strong, strong hands with veins that worked, magic fingers that ran up and down his slender instrument.

'I was at the concert with my first husband. We'd been having a rough patch. Our last rough patch. He was buying me back with trips out – concerts, meals, theatres. For this concert I was sitting there with a whole heap of arum lilies. I'd been feeling a bit daft with them. They're not the sort of thing you can carry discreetly at a swish function. I'd even thought about going to the ladies' in the interval to get shut. Imagine going to the loo and finding arum lilies sprouting out!

'But I forgot all about them when the clarinet man came out and started to play. They lay limp on my lap and my chest rose and fell in time with him pursing his lips to blow. I think my husband just thought I was enjoying his company. He was like that.'

You were laughing harder now, I noticed. Chelsea had a cherry up each of her boyfriend's nostrils and whipped cream shaped into a beard for him. Everyone was a bit tiddly so they were laughing. So was he and trying to lick it off. Everyone was glad Chelsea had decided to see a nice policeman. He was obviously good-natured. We were pleased – although we wouldn't dare say so – because she had packed in a long-running do with a patient of hers. He had vanished.

'When the concert ended, my clarinet man had to play the last few notes. He was the star of the show. I forget what the piece was. Usually I never know when a piece ends. How *do* people tell? On the radio it always takes me by surprise. The audiences sound very well informed. I'd be scared I'd jump up too early, clapping and making a show of myself. But this time there was no doubt. My man had put the most exquisite finishing touches on the whole extravaganza and, all at once, we all jumped to our feet to applaud and applaud.

'And suddenly I knew exactly what I was to do with my arum lilies. It came to me in a flash. I'd seen the type of thing on the telly with ballerinas and opera singers. I hoisted up my armful of flowers, pushed past my husband and along the aisle. Everyone still clapping, some of them watching me with eyebrows raised as I pelted down the steps towards the orchestra pit.

'It obviously wasn't the done thing. But I didn't care. The last thing I saw was my clarinet man, taking in the applause with a modest grin. He bowed, rose up, and looked stunned to see me heading his way. I must have been shocking, I suppose. But when I put my mind to it I can be impetuous.

'I slipped. I flew down half the aisle's steps. Arum lilies everywhere, pattering down on musicians' heads.

'I hit the pit with a sickening crash.

'Silence. And then pandemonium. Everyone came running, my husband among them. In my daze I could hear him shouting, even above all the noise. But it was my lovely clarinetist who reached down for me first, setting his shining instrument aside. I had broken both my legs in numerous places. The agony was considerable.'

She fell quiet for a moment and watched this sink in.

What do you say? You want to ask if that's why she has a cane now, but you can't. And meanwhile she rested both plump hands on her stick, looked away and smugly inspected the rest of the party before going on.

'I was in plaster for months and months. Right up to my navel and I'm still not right. You wouldn't believe the itches. And how clammy you get when it isn't even warm out. Have you ever been in plaster?'

I was thinking that she couldn't possibly have been in up to her navel. I mean, how did she . . . ? How could she manage to . . . ? Yet people get their whole bodies put in plaster sometimes. They must have to work something out. It's not as if you can suspend all bodily functions until you're on the mend. The body doesn't work like that, surely. Anyway, no, I told her, I'd never broken anything.

'Then you're very lucky. Although for me it was a blessing in disguise. My first visitor, after my husband – who just about said in as many words that it was all my own stupid fault – was the clarinetist. I lay back in traction, amazed. I could hardly say a word to him. He was charming, charming. The perfect bedside manner. He was under obligation, he said, to visit me on the orchestra's behalf and it was a pleasure, he added, a personal pleasure, to check up on the wellbeing of my legs. And he brought me some arum lilies. I was in heaven.

'After that he came every week. Until they went on tour and then it was every month and he would phone up from whichever concert hall he was appearing at. Sometimes, if he had his instrument with him, he would tootle a few notes down the line at me.'

She sighed.

'Eventually I was allowed to go home. I knew something was up when my husband never showed up on the Monday morning with the car. I stood in the foyer by the hospital flower shop and realised that he wasn't going to come at all. In a flash I saw that my husband had taken the opportunity to leave me. Well, I didn't mind really. The spark had long gone out of it and when he had visited me recently I was obviously elsewhere. I had been thinking about my clarinet man and where he would ring from next, even though he'd given me a tour itinerary and I knew where he would be until he returned. I called a taxi and went home by myself.

'Sure enough, my husband had taken everything of his out of the house. It looked very clean with half the pictures off the walls. I sat down and cried for a bit. Not for my husband. Not really. But because . . . because I had no one to write on my clean, clean plaster and because underneath it all I itched so terribly. I itched so much I could have bitten all the plaster away with my teeth just to be free. It felt so sticky and wet and yet, at the same time, dry and flaking too. As if my flesh underneath was turning to jelly, losing its form since it wasn't getting sunlight and exposure. In the narrow dark it was flaking apart and when they cut me loose I'd just fall to bits. Like those giant puffy fungus balls you find in the darkest corners of forests. Kick them and they explode into grey, slimy powder. So I cried in frustration and quite a bit of pain.

'Hang on.'

And suddenly Margaret was gone. She had noticed that the poet in her own right had left her deck chair. Some of the other poets had noticed this too and were looking about in consternation. There was to be a special presentation and they thought their leader had left before she could be given her crystal goblets and book voucher. The orange deck chair and glass looked sad and lost. I scratched my knee and shuffled on the concrete. It was starting to feel a bit clammy out. You came back.

'Jennifer's disappeared. They want to give her the presentation but they think she's slipped away without a fuss.'

I said, 'She's been crying all night.'

'She does this at the end of every term. After each reading.' You rolled your eyes. 'We're her ladies and we mightn't re-subscribe for the next course. Or if we do, it's never quite the same experience twice.'

'No.'

'We have to go quite soon.'

'Our coats will be under that big heap.'

'That's a point. Jennifer can't just have slunk off. She'd never find her mac without someone's help. Not in her state.'

Margaret appeared at the french windows. She resumed her place on the wall. 'They've found her. She'd passed out in the bathroom.'

'Oh, God!' you said. 'Well, we can't go until they've done the presentation. There was hell on when I left early last year. We're meant to be a *group*.'

Margaret said, 'I'm sure she won't take long to come round.' She said it just the way Chelsea had said the gateaux would soon defrost.

'Where was I?' asked Margaret.

'Up to your navel in plaster of Paris.'

You raised an eyebrow.

'Right. When his tour finished he came to see me. Armfuls of lilies. Chocolates and champagne aplenty.'

'He'd fallen in love with you, too.'

'That's quite right. It's very rare, in my experience, that a fairy tale comes quite so true. But in this one instance it certainly looked that way and every one of my feelings turned out to be mutual. Broken legs, ha! I'd have crawled over broken glass and he said he would as well. It's a rare thing, I'm telling you, and I'll tell you something else. When you get it, grab hold with both hands and don't you let go.'

'No,' I said, looking down.

'He gave me personal recitals,' said Margaret.

You turned away, your shoulders shaking with laughter.

'I'd sit with my aching heart and my itching lower body and legs in the swivel armchair he'd bought for my convenience and comfort and he'd play. All sorts of wonderful, haunting pieces. He'd play so long we wouldn't notice the dark steal in around us. It'd be night-time in a flash. He would exhaust the repetoire of everything he knew by heart and he'd sit back, clutching that clarinet of his, puffed out.

'And my skin, plastered or otherwise, would always be thrilled.

'This went on for some time. I never got tired of the same old pieces. Well, you don't, do you? I did once ask if he played any other instrument. And he fixed me with that charismatic grin. God, he was too good to be true, that man. Too good for this world, he was.

'It turned out he played anything and everything in the woodwind section. He had a natural gift. A real knack. Anything with holes and a place to blow down.

'It got so that he'd bring a different instrument round each night and we'd have the same tunes. But each time sounding slightly different through something new. Piccolos, recorders, saxophones, even, on one memorable occasion, a kazoo. Which between his lips sounded heavenly.

'When he played I would weep. Out of love and pleasure and – I think he must have realised – frustration. I'd lose myself in music and, without realising, thrash about on my swivel chair. He'd play even harder, with greater gusto, more beautifully than ever and then I would sob much deeper.

'Then one night he came and he took out of his carrying case something I didn't recognise as a musical instrument at all. I watched dumbfounded as he set it up, with a little smile. Unwound a flex. Plugged it in.'

At this point the poet in her own right reappeared on the Tuscany patio. Back on her feet and surrounded by friends, Chelsea most prominent among them, clutching goblet-shaped parcels. Jennifer's hair was stuck down wetly on her forehead. She'd had her face splashed with cold water. It was down the front of her blouse.

'Speech! Speech!' the poets cried and everyone clapped.

As Jennifer struggled for a few words with which to end the current term of workshops and round off the whole evening, you were poking in your handbag for your car keys, hoping for a quick getaway. Margaret hissed the rest of the story.

'A Black and Decker drill. He'd had to buy it new. My husband took ours with him.'

'What did the clarinetist want with one? What did he do with it?'

'A fair-sized hole at the end of my big toe on the left foot. Then thirty smaller, at regular intervals, all the way up to my navel.

'Then he lay on the floor beneath me and I sat back on my swivel chair and waited.

'Sheer bloody poetry he gave me and it's honestly worth the itching if you can get it scratched by a virtuoso.'

The Giant Spider's Supervisor

As usual we were playing on the back of the giant spider. One of those games where your feet can't touch the ground. You're dead if your feet touch tarmac. Imagine the sizzle, scalded rubber, of plimsolls on hot, pink playground tarmac.

Mind, lots of the kids turn up barefoot, or in sandals. Unsuitably attired. The parents send them any old how, just getting them off their hands. Sending babies, too. We get kids bringing younger ones in pushchairs. Of course we have to send them back.

But I'm starting at the point with us all on the giant spider's back. Each of its – how many? Six – legs was a ladder to the thick red abdomen I was straddling, shouting, 'Quick, run! Quick! So the spider can take off!' And the kids were screaming, scrambling aboard, because they didn't want to be left behind.

You have to make all sorts of stuff up. This giant spider can fly anywhere if I say so. They look up to me, even when I'm not towering above them, straddling the red abdomen of the giant spider in my cut-off jeans, my white cotton shirt knotted at my waist, a paisley scarf keeping my hair out of my eyes while I work. Though at its best it's hardly work. I don't wear sunglasses, although we've had some lovely days already this summer, because they tend to alienate the bairns. I think that's what put them off Marsha, actually.

Marsha's leaving put me in charge, made me sole supervisor. So we come here, most days, to sit on the giant spider with the six laddered legs. When I say so it can take us where we like.

Some of my kids stayed on the swings. Wedged in truck tyres, heaving themselves high as they could go. Refusing to give up their precious places even for a go on the spider.

When we're in the park they all enjoy themselves and fling themselves into it. Our enjoyment this summer is headlong and reckless. But each has one ear open, waiting for me to yell that the spider is powering up, readying to leave without us. They are tensed to catch up, these bairns.

'Where's he going today, the giant spider?' I ask.

Jackie answers, a girl who's so white she looks like a skeleton and has purple rings around her eyes. They can't be bruises unless terrible trouble has been taken to make them in that shape. She goes, 'I think the spider's going to Jurassic Park.'

All the other kids go 'Yeah!' and there's an excitement as everyone realises what she's said, punching of shoulders, kids pretending to be dinosaurs.

'What do you want to go there for?'

'I don't,' Jackie goes. 'It's just where the spider's going today.'

I decide I don't want to go to Jurassic Park today, actually. We've had three weeks on this play scheme and not a day's gone by without dinosaurs in some form. Me, I like the giant spider, its thick red abdomen, the splayed green, laddered legs. That blistered paintwork with writing gouged in by house keys. I wonder who here is of reading age and, if so, whether they can read the *Lara's a Slag*, *Stew's Ugly as Fuck*, *Michael Summers Sucks Cock* and *We Did an E Here 93* on the skin of the spider that's meant to carry them to Jurassic Park.

I go, 'I know.' (I slipped into prefacing everything I say with 'I know' weeks ago, as if everything was spontaneous.) 'Why doesn't the giant spider take a swim under the ocean?'

'Like in *The Little Mermaid*,' Susan coos. She wants to be the Little Mermaid because she's ginger. She sings all the songs in this chilling, raspy voice and it makes me sad for her. Don't know why; probably because she's so ugly, poor bairn. That prized red hair looks like it's been washed and clotted up with house soap.

'Crap!' This is Daniel, who looks at me narrowly because the giant spider wants to go under the ocean again. As sole interpreter of the giant spider's wishes, suddenly I'm under Daniel's suspicions.

When the giant spider is under the ocean I lie on my back and make everyone pretend to be a fish or a starfish for an hour or more. It's dead relaxing. Daniel isn't the only dissenter. There were a few tuts when I said the bottom of the ocean again. They're getting bored, I see. I no longer have them in the palm of my hand. With this tide turning maybe it'll be Jurassic Park after all.

Susan can switch from Little Mermaid simper to vitriol in seconds flat. 'I bet Daniel wants to go to Tracey Island really,' she spat. Awkward on the spider's laddered legs, she was showing her knickers as she tried to get her balance. 'Yeh. Go to Tracey Island, Daniel. To be with the . . . Thunderbirds!' She shrieks with laughter.

Daniel colours and the other kids are laughing now. It's true, I realise, he does look like a puppet and the cruel little buggers have picked up on this. 'I don't! I don't want to fuckin' be a Thunderbird!'

There's a sharp 'Eeee!' from most of the group. I decided at the start not even to blink should 'fuck' get said on this scheme. You just can't stop it. A blind eye costs nothing, but I draw the line at 'cunt' and there has been one or two of those.

To start with, Marsha was our leader this summer. She's gone now and good riddance, I say. She was much too *busy* for me. Small wonder the council made her play-scheme supervisor. They recognised something in her, a restless and commandeering energy. Bossy, I call it. She always had to be up and at 'em. It was something new every five minutes. Never a moment's rest and it got on my nerves, me starting this job and thinking I was on to a cushy number. Even the poor bairns were going home knackered by teatime.

Rounders out on the playing field for the whole afternoon, that's what Marsha liked. Nonstop rounders, mind. That terrible version of the game in which, if someone's struck off, you've only got the time of the protesting scream that goes up to grab the flung-down bat if you're next in line and get struck off yourself. The tennis ball gets chucked at your wicket without you when you're not fast enough. Marsha liked this breakneck version because it kept everyone engaged and concentrating all afternoon. And it did, it did, I have to admit, but I went home with my shoulders and arms like a lobster and my knees actually shook as if I'd been kicked, after all that dashing about.

Horrible Ruby, the gingham-smocked caretaker of the community centre where our scheme is housed when the days are raining, came to the doors to watch us play, to make sure we weren't ruining the council's equipment. She snapped a fag in and out of her mouth, smoking efficiently, using a blue bucket as an ashtray and saying to me as I wandered over, glad of the break, 'That Marsha's a miracle worker, isn't she? Getting those scruffy bairns playing a fair game all afternoon. The bairns round here'd be running wild without her.'

There was no sitting on the back of the giant spider all afternoon with Marsha.

Once we had an inspection to see how we were getting on and a bloke turned up in a car. But we were out. We had walked all forty of our kids across town in a godawful raucous convoy. Over three main roads and honest, I think about it now and we could have lost or killed any number of them. Little bastards running off and tearing about as we walked alongside the rank Burn. They went wild in the trees, in the mottled blue shadows down the Burn. Marsha strode ahead. She made a stick for herself, stripping leaves and bark off a slender branch and she swished it along. Not a care in the world. Assured that everyone was behaving themselves. I was bringing up the rear, sweating.

*   *   *

For this job, which ends in September, the council pays me fifty pounds a week. Although I am paid to entertain the kiddies and keep them off the streets, I realise now what I am really being paid for.

1) Taking the blame should any child on the estates our scheme caters for be killed this summer by a car or a pervert or another kid or whatever. Because there is a scheme, there ought to be no casualties. They are catered for. I am a caterer. The parents are customers, with a right to complain if their kids are damaged. The parents here shove their kids out their doors at eight in the morning, take them in again at night-time, later as summer advances. It would be like this even without a scheme nearby. The scheme is convenient for emergencies. The same parents send two-year-old, three-year-old bairns in pushchairs. Our posters say six to twelve. We get the extremes; the insensible babies and the bored teenagers lolling over fences, gobbing and leering at us, wanting, really, to join in, I reckon.

2) Our bodies, as supervisors, sun-branded and sore and toughened from days out in the sullied air, are rented out to kids half our age. We are walking climbing frames. On walks they cling to our arms, dangle from us, clamber round our necks; they follow us about and are familiar with us. We're not like teachers and they take pride in knowing us by our first names. We are older brothers and sisters to them; they take our hands, wait to delight in hearing us swear by mistake. They take a keen interest in progress made by Neil and Michelle, helpers with another scheme across town. Everyone knows they've been fucking since June and suddenly Michelle is having a bairn of her own.

It's later summer now and, if anything, hotter than ever. I've not known a season last as long as this since I was a bairn. Being out in it all so much makes me feel I've wrung every drop from it. Like the precious days on the estate, down the Burn, when I was about ten, say. Summer a long season then, everything reeking of dog shit because people take their dogs on longer walks and the shit gets spread that much further afield. The company of children gives me back an illusion of a lifetime in the sun. I've gone a glorious suntanned colour; pale old me, it's incredible. Especially since so much of the time we've spent underwater. This afternoon we are under the ocean once more. I managed to talk them out of Jurassic Park. Which last time gave me a headache, actually.

Martin hasn't been on the giant spider today. He kept his place on the swings, doggedly as if he thought it was doing him some good. A few minutes ago he left his swing to its own devices and he went sniffing round the brick pavilion at the back of us.

The brick pavilion is disused and dark. I remember it as having an ice-cream counter inside. A window with an old woman squirting yellow Mr Whippy out of a machine. There were toilets. One of those swinging signs outside for Lyon's Maid; a picture of three kids skipping, holding hands. Now every window and door is boarded up and painted blue.

While we're relaxed and still in our under-ocean routine on the giant spider, Martin gives a yell and comes running out of the brick pavilion. We sit up muggy and confused like sleepers. What if someone really falls asleep some day and they drop right off onto tarmac? Ours isn't one of those parks Esther Rantzen converted with woodchips for safety.

'Come and see!' Martin's yelling. He wears a T-shirt from the Tuesday market, navy blue with a clumsy transfer that reads, 'Take That!' I saw them on sale, two quid each, last week. This summer has been slippery with the nylon sheen of T-shirts bought in Aycliffe market.

'What is it?' I dredge myself from the silty bed to meet a cobalt sky tight as Tupperware. I haven't put on my supervisor voice. 'What is it, Martin?' I try again, brassy, bright.

When I ease down off the giant spider, the legs are hot on my bare skin. Martin takes my hand in his. It's unlike him, he's eight and usually pushing off ahead like a real little lad. 'What is it?' I ask and he's pulling me to visit the brick pavilion. My mouth's gone dry and the other kids have picked up on Martin's unnerving quiet and the fact that it's freaking me out. They are coming along with us, into the sheltered concrete space which reeks of dry piss, Martin urging us into the space behind the rosehip bushes. In here it's shadowed and cooler and I'd say creepy. I'd warn Martin not to come in. Imagine if the likes of our play scheme didn't go on. Imagine where Martin would play.

I ask, 'What have you found?' and make sure the others hang back a suitable distance. They do, knowing something weird is up and not wanting to see it too close, which is my job, after all. I'm being paid to come between them and whatever weird and hazardous thing it is Martin's discovered in the boarded-up brick pavilion.

Wordlessly he points to the stained boards over what used to be Mr Whippy's counter. Among the graffiti and scars there's a dark strip which, as I approach, I see is a letterbox slot of darkness, about head height with Martin.

I swallow my breath whole, fight down my pulse rate and take three steps forwards. I bend and glare into the hole in the boards and find I'm glaring straight into an unblinking eye. I can see it's surrounded by puckers of grey flesh. It has no brows or lashes and it's threaded with a painful number of scarlet capillaries. Besides this I can see nothing else in the gap.

Horrible Ruby told us later that she had dealt with the man from the council herself. He'd arrived in a big car with smoked windows and even a little flag. She went out in her gingham smock and carried her broom with her. It was a real caretaker's broom, its bristled head three feet across.

'They're all out,' she shouted to the council man. 'You can't inspect them because Marsha's taken them all roller-skating for the afternoon.'

The man from the council reportedly frowned. 'The rink is across the other side of town.'

'They walk it no bother,' Ruby went. 'They're all young, aren't they?'

We were crossing three main roads in that hectic croco-dile. I look back now, appalled at Marsha's stick-swishing insouciance, but also at my discomforted complacency in leaving it all up to her.

We were walking alongside the rank Burn, right across town, two by two, singing songs. This is the first summer in years I've known all the songs in the top ten. I'm out of date at twenty.

'This sounds enterprising of Marsha,' said the councillor.

'It's all free at the open-air rink across town,' said Ruby. 'They have a lovely time. Every time they come back full of it.'

'I'm glad to see the scheme such a success this year.'

'Oh, yes.' Horrible Ruby approved. 'That Marsha has her head screwed on.'

At the open-air rink, across the road from the borstal, everything was free, even hiring your roller boots. Most of the time I spent on my knees, going through piles of leathery-smelling boots, combining sizes and tying the squirming bairns' laces. Setting them off with a soft push onto the smooth concrete. The little wheels, all combined, set up a hum of gentle thunder.

I rarely got to have a go myself and when I did, because it was an old pair, somebody else's broken-in boots, I got a terrible blood blister under one heel. It went to the size of half an apple and I couldn't stand on that foot for a week. When it popped – on a rainy day indoors – bad blood spilled out on the parquet floor and, oddly, it smelled like shit. Horrible Ruby shot out with her dustpan, fussing about, and dumped a heap of sawdust on the mess. I wasn't ashamed as I might have been had it not been an injury I'd received in the work I was doing.

I felt slightly aggrieved that I couldn't skate more often. I used to be a dab hand. At ten I taught myself on the smooth roads of our local streets. I had a shopping trolley we'd fished out of the Burn; I used to push myself round in that. Don't ask me why or how. There's a photo of me doing that somewhere, stuck out in the middle of the road. Honestly; slumped inside a shopping trolley with my legs hanging out to pedal on tarmac. Like an underprivileged bairn with nothing better to play on.

Meanwhile Marsha was skating, easily and cleverly, about the stained concrete rink. And all the kids followed her round in bright circles, a leisurely hurricane.

I think fast this afternoon, backing away from the blue boards in the brick pavilion.

'Let me see,' urge the bairns' voices, 'let me see,' and their bodies push forwards, eager since I'm so quiet about what I've glimpsed. Only Martin, I notice, is still, with his arms crossed.

I think fast this afternoon, though, using the skills I've picked up already this summer. And one of the first, most important things I discovered was ways of deflecting, of catching up in a handful and redirecting attention. So with a clattering new brightness in my voice I make this moment turn a letter L.

'I know!' I cry, startling them all. 'The giant spider is taking off again! He's leaving the bottom of the ocean – listen!' And they're all listening now as if spider language comes broadcast. 'Listen!' I add a tremor of excitement. 'He's flying to Jurassic Park!'

They yelp and bicker and pelt their way back to the spider on the pink asphalt park. Up the metal legs they scamper before the spider can take off. Again I bring up the rear and Martin lags alongside me. His whole face is eyeing me and he won't conspire in my forced change of mood.

We would meet the other schemes at places like the Recreation Centre, up by the industrial estate. Another perilous walk across town, this time through an underpass. It was on these trips we all took an interest in Neil and Michelle, how they were fucking and how Michelle's foetus was faring. Were the facts of life something else we were paid fifty quid to impart?

We gave the children free rein on the Rec's assault course. When four schemes from separate estates met up on an afternoon there were round about two hundred kids. It was mental and most of the supervisors sloped off and left them to it.

The supervisors would have a smoke together. Michelle and Neil would be our centrepiece for some reason. As if we were all basking in their fecund glow. When the kids came over with scuffed knees or grievances, they always talked to Neil and Michelle first, as if they'd become parents to all of us overnight.

While we sat on the grassy bank and smoked and left the bairns to the assault course, Marsha would be standing up high on a wall, blowing a whistle and screaming instructions at two hundred kids.

'Listen to her!' Neil scowled.

'She's keen,' said Michelle.

And I was embarrassed because we were partners. I had to work doubly hard to make myself cool because of Marsha.

Robin said, 'The kids hate her, too.'

'They take the piss out of her,' said Joanne.

'She's going to university, isn't she?' asked Michelle. 'Isn't that right?' she asked me.

'How the fuck should I know?'

'You work with her.'

At that point I was getting shit from all sides. At the end of that afternoon Marsha took me aside at the mouth of the underpass and, within hearing of the bairns, said sedately but with venom, 'Get your finger out or I'll have you sacked, Teresa.'

I went back after work. I had to see again. But I couldn't let any of the kids see where I was going, so I hung on in the community centre until I was sure they'd be long gone. Horrible Ruby ambled up.

'You'll be pleased with yourself, being supervisor now.'

'I've been surpervisor a couple of weeks already. Since Marsha went.'

'Hm.' She looked me up and down. 'And do you really think the kids are still enjoying the scheme?'

136

'I hope so.'

'You're not putting in half as much effort as poor Marsha did. Them bairns aren't getting their money's worth out of you. I've seen you, up at the park all day. Just sitting on the giant spider.'

I scowled. 'They don't pay for it anyway.'

'Their parents pay taxes.'

'No, they don't.'

I left then and went straight back to the park, which was deserted, and to the brick pavilion, which was even more eerie. I steeled myself in the pissy concrete alcove behind the rosehip bushes and again I peered into the letterbox in the boards. That eye was still looking back, almost placidly.

I turned and ran all the way home, as I hadn't since I was a kid myself, hounded home from school by the threat of a scrap.

What happened next was that Marsha went too far and she must have been too cocky for her own good. Because the next thing I knew she was flat on her arse in the middle of the outdoor rink, in the eyes of the cackling tornado.

I'm not saying did she fall or was she pushed, but just beforehand I'd heard Robin and Michelle and Neil talking about how snotty and ugly she looked, zipping round and round on the concrete, and then Michelle went out onto the rink. Actually Marsha looked the very opposite of ugly. I'm no fan but I have to admit she looked nice, especially that day. I was on the benches as usual, matching one pair of boots with another, the knuckle-bruising business of unpicking laces that have begun to rot.

Marsha was flung somehow through a gap that opened obligingly in the bank of skaters behind her and against the chest-high wall at the side. She hit the deck with a dismayed shriek and an arm broken in three places. From the benches I saw it flop about horribly and it took some moments for everyone to stop skating. Only when there was silence and we were all staring down at Marsha, on the floor in her yellow dungarees, did she burst into tears.

'It's my left arm!' she was sobbing when the ambulance crew arrived with their blankets and started calling everyone 'love' in that softly bossy way they have. 'I'm an artist! It's my left arm!'

And it was true. She was due to go to art college in Newcastle this autumn. That was buggered up. After three days Marsha returned to work with a plaster cast that made her teeth grit each time she moved it. By her return I'd already picked up the reins on our scheme. Marsha should have realised. Those had been her rules in nonstop rounders and now the baton was mine.

For a couple of days she took a back seat and once I saw her trying to sketch something in a pad with her plastered arm. We were up at the park. My idea; I had all of the kids up on the back of the giant spider. It was our first flight clinging to his laddered legs and his red abdomen and poor Marsha was relegated to watching, trying to draw us. I saw her try and fail miserably. The next day up at the assault course she couldn't blow her whistle and wave her arms like a slave driver. She had to ride out the other supervisors' lazy mockery.

And then, suddenly, Marsha left. She gave in her notice and didn't come back.

After that we went all over the place on the back of the giant spider. But mostly we went to the bottom of the sea. The bairns were happy. They couldn't remember a time without the giant spider, without the green laddered legs, the thick red abdomen, the afternoons spent lazily at the bottom of the sea.

By August's end none of them even remembered Marsha and how the summer began. Summer this year was spent on the giant spider's back.

And as August played itself out I began to miss the whole thing before the event. Everything took on a certain tinge. Up at the assault course we heard that Neil was marrying Michelle. Because of their bairn on the way they'd get a house, no bother. They were lucky. I got a silly crush on that Andrew for a bit, but that fell through. I think it was just

138

the bairns urging me on with their bizarre sense of symmetry and anyway, I think he was queer. The bairns had a laugh, they played and fought and there were a few minor mishaps, only one major one, when Horrible Ruby got pushed over by accident when she was out by the community-centre bins. She brushed herself down, shaken and furious, and I apologised effusively, promising to give Martin a good talking-to.

Horrible Ruby just gave me a sickly, triumphant smile. 'It doesn't matter,' she said. 'I know it won't happen again. And it definitely won't happen again next year, will it?'

It turned out the skating injury was worse than anyone imagined and Marsha and her parents were suing the council for the loss of her artistic arm and her place at art college in Newcastle. In view of that the council was dropping all future schemes. Horrible Ruby filled me in on this gossip beside the community-centre bins while the kids around us blinked, half understanding, fascinated by the trickle of blood coming from Ruby's nose. Next year seemed so far away. Could they even see a time so far away?

Things stop being prosaic and normal when it seems that they're coming to an end. How many more trips on the back of the giant spider?

Not many. Then I was back on the income support and the kids at school again.

I'd go past the park every now and then. On the way to the shops, usually; not on the way back. I'd look silly sitting alone on the spider's back with a bagful of groceries. I'd sit for a while.

During late Indian summer, through mid-autumn, then the early, circumspect days of winter, the giant spider never felt like travelling anywhere.

Each time I checked on the spider I'd check on the brick pavilion too. In the alcove behind the rosehip bushes I'd gather my nerve and bend to peer in through the dark gap.

Whoever it was still looked out at me each time. By the end of the year I'd started to find that oddly reassuring, actually.

THOSE IMAGINARY COWS

EITHER I STAYED where I was and endured another end-of-party 4.00 a.m. showing of *Room with a View*, or I pursued the repressed Catholic boy I had earlier propositioned to his hiding place upstairs, or I went out into the garden for a smoke with Esmé.

Outside it was spitting on to rain and the garden furniture glowed like old bones on the lawn.

Esmé's stark bald head swayed and bobbed across the table from me. She lit our cigarettes, poured more wine, and launched stridently into complaints about Michael, her new lover. As if the neighbours couldn't hear, and as if I had known her for years, which I hadn't.

I've heard all this before, I thought. Maybe I should have told her at the start about Michael.

She was an American friend. In my experience Americans have made friends with me quite easily and quickly. Often without my being aware of the fact. All it took in Esmé's case was a quick introduction. She found me suitably acerbic and quaint, and she was flattered by my pointing out that she must be named after a Lolita in a Salinger story or a hyena in one by Saki. After that we were best buddies and almost immediately she began taking liberties.

One night when the telly wouldn't come on she got on to talking about sex.

She was a dancer and general physical performance artiste, so she was sitting on the floor. She propped her recently shaved head on her hands, delicately rested her elbows on my knees and asked if I thought anal intercourse was passé.

This was the beginning of our period of intimacy. Which ended – in as much as such intimacies can ever end – with my punching her in the mouth in an effort to restore her to life.

'I wouldn't go in for it again,' I said, thinking that would be an end to the matter.

'Me neither,' she said, nodding. 'It sucks.' She laughed and stopped abruptly, giving me an appraising stare. 'I knew you were gay. I was talking to Michael about it, but he wouldn't say anything. I mean, it isn't that you're camp or anything . . .'

She let it tail away. She pronounced 'camp' with a drawling vowel, as if there were an *h* in it. Her accent, a sunny Denver-Colorado staccato, was drenched already with mismatched vowel sounds she assumed were English. Eventually she came out of her year abroad sounding, as well as looking, quite deranged.

Michael, I reflected, certainly wouldn't say anything about me. Esmé was reaching for my cigarettes with a customary inverse hospitality which enabled her to grab what she required qualm-free.

So. Anal intercourse sucked. I wondered if she knew yet – I presumed she didn't – that Michael did too.

Then came the revelation meant to bond us in complicity. 'I can tell you this, since I know you'll understand.'

I nodded grimly and thought about how much more attractive she had been upon first arriving, when she was all Louise Brooks hair and public-theatre workshops. In one of those workshop sessions she had met Michael. She shaved her head to be like him and nowadays they meditated and wrestled together in the formation of a performance aesthetic of their own. I wouldn't have minded so much if they didn't work on it in the room above mine.

She said, 'I'm a bisexual butterfly.'

I was more surprised at the second bit.

Esmé went to the corner shop for some wine and we

christened our complicity and superiority well into the early
hours of that night. By the time I stumbled into my room
and threw up purple on the carpet, I had told her the ins
and outs of everything.

She had dragged on thirteen of my fags; eyes alive and
magnified in her granny glasses at each salacious gem of
conversation, starting in genuine interest only once, when I
told her that I had fucked Michael too.

'It was over a year ago. I doubt he remembers it.'

'But he does,' she asserted. 'He told me about it.'

'What were you on about before, then? You were talking
as if Michael was the straightest thing on earth.'

'He is straight,' she told me, very seriously. 'But you are
a very, very special person.'

I went to my room and, as I said, threw up on the floor.

This night, though, in the dark at the cast-iron garden
table, with the drizzle diluting our wine and running down
our faces, Esmé was showing none of that easy, carefree
glamour of our earlier friendship. She was miserable as
sin. Our pre-empted intimacy had lost its atmosphere of
sophomore slumber party and gained a kind of extravagant
despair. Esmé was given to theatricals.

'You must tell me,' she burst out, 'how much he still thinks
of her.'

'How should I know how much? She'll still be on his mind
– she's bound to be . . .'

'She' was Michael's last girlfriend, Jackey, another friend
of mine. That was a friendship a long time in the making,
through much mutual suspicion, circumspection and the
added complications of mine and Michael's goings-on at
the time. I wasn't about to commit myself on anything to
do with Jackey for Esmé's benefit. In this case, I realised,
Esmé was expendable. Whatever she showered me with –
genuine or not – I didn't owe her anything.

She pulled her face into a leering frown. She was very pale
and even-featured. There was a calm blankness about her that
could, at times, make her seem beautiful. But I had begun to

suffer the first symptoms of a falling-out. Esmé was looking
more hideous, to my eyes at least, with each passing crisis.

'They had a real Brontë thing going for them,' I said. 'It
was all passion and tears and banging on windows.'

'Do you think he wants to go back with her?'

'She's living right across the country now.'

'Catherine Earnshaw was dead. She can catch the train at
any time!'

'Jackey has other things to do now. I don't suppose she
would ever want to get wrapped back up in a poisonous
affair with Michael. She's grown out of him.'

Esmé looked stung and for a moment I was pleased. Then
I wondered, how much had I grown up?

The following teatime I watched Michael cooking. Staring
gloomily at the filthy work surfaces, I downed a bottle of
Bulgarian red and we talked. His newly sprouting head was
nodding deliberately over the chopping board. He hacked
his thick-fingered way through yellow peppers, courgettes,
onions. Vegetarian cookery depresses me after a while.
There are only so many nights a week you can relish your
virtuousness; frying up the same old pulpy faces, rearranging
your spices for maximum interest.

Esmé had already arrived home. Today she was moving
in, with her luggage in extraordinary hatboxes, her extraordinary hats squashed in a repulsive pile on her head. Michael
was serving up a special meal in celebration, but they had
argued as soon as her Doc Martens hit our tea-stained
lino. Esmé wanted to commemorate Thanksgiving with us
by cooking a special Mexican meal. She had a bagful of
ingredients, but Michael had got there first.

'Thanksgiving for what?' he grunted, square-shouldered,
unsure, deep-set eyes wriggling backwards like twin conga eels.

At first she refused to argue. 'It's my culture,' she said
primly, fluffing up the peacock feathers stuck out of her
Saks carrier bag. 'If I'm going to live here, you ought to
respect my culture.'

Michael was making jasmine tea. He turned back savagely

to the mugs. 'Respect the slaughter of an indigenous population?' His voice was stammering and thick, as if he had eaten four Mars bars on the trot. The tea leaves were in a tiny stainless-steel house on the end of a chain. He swirled this in the mugs, passed me mine. It looked diseased.

After a significant pause he told Esmé, 'You can cook what you fucking well like – but I'm not eating it if it means giving thanks to America.'

She seized her luggage to her. 'I miss my family!' she cried brokenly. 'I'll miss our turkey this year!'

We watched her turn, march smartly out of the kitchen, across the dark-brown living room – where the others were watching *Countdown* – and up the wooden stairs to, presumably, Michael's bedroom.

He went back to his cooking. In the end I said, 'Couldn't you put some Mexican spices in it, to make her feel better?'

'She isn't even from Mexico.'

'I know, but it might cheer her up.'

He deliberated. 'She'd only say it was too weak.'

I had already heard about Esmé's early years in Mexico. Her parents had done a hippy thing. Her father taught creative writing to convicts and they had eventually moved back to Colorado in time for Esmé to do a Goth thing; working in a boutique, selling 'antique vintage dresswear' to other Goths.

On the face of it, Esmé had rather a lot in common with Jackey. Jackey wore black leather and leggings, was six foot two with pomegranate-coloured hair at least half that length and a drop-dead look that teetered in intensity between the Bride of Dracula and Paddington's Aunt Lucy. She was also piss-your-pants funny, which was why, with head swollen and knocking drunkenly already, I was pleased to answer the door while Michael dunked chilli powder into his wok, to find Jackey framed there, arms flung wide, teeth bared, ready for a surprise visit.

'Ha ha ha ha!'

Michael groaned, 'Oh, fuck!' and by accident dropped the whole jar of cayenne into Esmé's supper.

*   *   *

I sat with Jackey on the park bench we had along one wall of the living room to watch *Top of the Pops*, and I explained how it had been easier to steal a bench than to clean the heaps of crap off the other chairs.

'I live with animals,' I said, and she tutted consolingly.

Michael and Esmé were arguing behind the shut kitchen door. At first it was about Esmé's dietary prohibitions – she saw broccoli bobbing in the wok and screeched about an aversion to tree vegetables – but now they were arguing about Jackey's presence. We did our level best to ignore it, for manners' sake. The family in the two-bedroom flat behind the wall on the other side were rowing also. We could hear them clearly through the bolted door that segregated us. Esmé had nailed one of her black winding sheets to the door to muffle the sound, but it didn't work.

Jackey was telling me about Leeds; about being part of a theatre company that was a Going Concern.

'The bastards won't give you the bookings. If you haven't been injured on *Casualty* or something exotic on *Blake's Seven* you don't get so much as a sniff of a stage.'

The kitchen door banged open and Michael stormed through, glared at us both, shot upstairs.

'He can fuck off as well,' Jackey muttered and rummaged in her pockets for cigarettes.

'That's not a vegetarian jacket.'

'I've given that stuff up,' she said. 'He tortured me over all that. About all the meat I'd eaten before I had my consciousness raised. He really played with my mind, that fucker. That afternoon we dropped acid in his favourite childhood haunt, when I was staying with his family, he really made me paranoid. Until the effects wore off, after twenty hours, I was plagued everywhere I went by imaginary cows. He loves doing that sort of thing to women.'

I fell silent, deciding not to defend him. We could see Esmé through the half-open kitchen door, sobbing against the freezer unit. We watched some rap artist on *Top of the Pops* – the third that edition – reiterating herself to a backing track.

Jackey sighed and changed the subject decisively, exclaiming, 'I hate that music. I bet she's a bloody American.'

I saw Esmé's back stiffen. Jackey clamped a hand to her mouth. She smudged lipstick all over the place as she suppressed a dangerous cackle.

After a few tense seconds, a silent Esmé followed Michael upstairs.

Our bathroom was comprehensively filmed with a fine white powder, impossible to remove. When the shower had leaked through crevices onto the noisy family below, the landlord had seen to it by having a tiled, waist-high wall built next to the bath. We assumed the stubborn coating everywhere had something to do with his grouting. The wall was a talking point. The theatre group had organised a party in its honour, during which it was examined, praised and christened (in semi-digested cheesecake, as I remember).

Before going out that evening, I was sitting on our wall, having my make-up seen to by Esmé. I pursed everything, intent on the delicate shovelling of mascara.

'It's a pity Michael looked like Frankenstein.'

'Frankenstein's monster,' I corrected, without moving my fuchsia lips.

'He needn't have washed it off.' She glanced at the dead colours streaking the sink.

'If you're going somewhere with the intention of looking conspicuous, you have to look fabulous as well.'

'Be quiet while I retouch your lips.'

'Can I light a fag?'

'No.' She dabbed me with a handkerchief, face held close, already made up and as lifeless in its concentration as the blunt end of a hammer. 'Both you and Michael have those funny, pretty rosebud lips. Very twenties. Yours are charming because they're slightly crooked.'

'That's where I got punched once.'

'Cheekbones,' she reminded us and began to dust me vigorously in grey.

From my room next door there came the muffled thumps

146

and curses of Jackey getting ready. My room had a huge window, three storeys up, overlooking a crossroads on a hill, the whole town spread below it. Jackey would be undressing, flinging clothes around for the benefit of everyone outside. Her motto: If you've got it, hang it out the window.

Esmé's hand trembled, finding a place for a beauty spot. 'Are you all right?'

Of course I felt hypocritical asking. Ten minutes earlier I had been bursting with silent laughter, with Jackey in my room. We had been taking the piss out of the bald people upstairs. Jackey had made a show of listening to and recognising the sounds of argument; Michael's gruff incoherence, the shriek of his bookshelves being wrenched out of the wall. The grinding bedsprings of reconciliation had wiped the smile off Jackey's face and replaced it with an expression of a different kind of memory.

I put *Hatful of Hollow* on and, minutes later, Esmé was banging on my door.

'That was quick.' Jackey was smirking again.

Esmé came humbly to offer her making-up services. Jackey gave her a sickly smile and I just gave myself up.

Now here was Esmé, flicking back tears, lip quivering. 'It's really hard for me,' she said, 'with Jackey here. I find her so difficult. Michael isn't happy about her coming out with us tonight.'

I thought about Michael, slumped upstairs in his post-coital squalor. I was never given to retribution, but at that moment I felt like kicking him soundly where he lay. No one like me had been there to watch *my* lip tremble over him. I thoroughly resented the spectacle of the three of us as three squabbling ex-shags, even if I didn't count. Especially when, really, he looked like a burglar's dog.

Michael was stubborn, though. Stubborn and squalid as his principles. He found every situation difficult and language jammed in his throat in situations like these. Yet he was hard-bitten, uncompromising. He was a former teenage star who, when appearing on *Blockbusters*, had taken as his mascot a Cornish pasty and insisted on answering with the most inappropriate words imaginable. Four years on, that subversive glamour had not faded. Recently, during one of Esmé's first nights in the house, we had watched his video of the show again. Esmé screamed with laughter at the sight of the seventeen-year-old Michael, with blond, already thinning hair, boyish without all his muscles, zapping the buzzer and shouting, 'Gdansk', 'Thighs', 'Usurpation' and 'Copious' in a strangely deep voice.

'That was so funny I think I peed in my pants,' Esmé gasped when it finished.

Michael frowned at her. He frowned as heavily as he had the night she explained how she and her family stole leftover food from the dumper trucks at the back of supermarkets and gift-wrapped each other rocks for Christmas. There were times when he seemed disgusted by her. But looking at Esmé now, disconsolate on the toilet seat and packing her make-up bag, I didn't have the heart to tell her that.

Since, in the end, Michael was too upset and disturbed to leave the house, it was to be me, Jackey and Esmé going together to Butchers. 'You can both be my fag hags,' I said and it fell on the stony ground of the littered living room. Esmé went to phone for a taxi because I refused to walk across town in full make-up.

'But you don't look queer at all. You won't get beaten up.' Jackey passed me a hip flask. 'At most you look like a butch lesbian in drag.'

I chewed on that for a while, until Esmé came back. The atmosphere between them was strained until they both found something to laugh at. Jackey said that they had to get to like each other, in case I copped off with someone that night and they ended up having to come home together. I submitted to this implausible pleasantry, glad that the ice had at least stopped smoking.

Then Jackey asked Esmé something about America, and Esmé told her something about America. Probably about

148

things being bigger and less expensive than here. That was the usual drift.

'Yes,' Jackey said. 'Of course, we've heard all this before. Paul used to go out with an American. A lovely boy. It only lasted a month. He's in Colorado too, now, isn't he?'

'Yes,' I said, tight-lipped.

'It only lasted a month because his boyfriend had to go back after a year,' Esmé put in, defending me.

'It was tragic, really,' Jackey agreed. 'They only had four brief weeks.'

'I've heard all about it. You were there, weren't you?'

Jackey nodded solemnly. 'They made such a lovely couple.'

'And they were born on exactly the same day. I think there's something . . . almost spiritual about that.'

'The poor things!' Jackey sighed. 'And he's not very happy in Colorado, you know. Taking drugs, the last we heard. I think he's still missing him. And there was bugger all spiritual about it if you ask me.'

'I wish I'd been here to see it. I'd like to see Paul happy. He deserves to be, doesn't he?'

'Oh, yes. He's been unlucky in love.'

Mercifully the taxi horn honked out in the street. I stood up, monumentally pissed off. 'Can we go now?' I strode out to the car looking, presumably, like an exquisitely petulant corpse.

'The Butchers, please,' I commanded, climbing in, and refused to acknowledge the driver's knowing wink.

The trouble started at the door. Jackey caused a fuss because she refused to say what she 'identified as' to the bouncer. I had already signed my name and number in the book and was squinting for a table into the low-ceilinged gloom.

'You must understand my difficulty,' the bouncer whined. 'This is an exclusive club.'

'What are you trying to say?' Jackey reared up.

'I mean, you don't look like a lesbian –'

She quivered with righteous, politically shit-hot indignation. I stepped in with umbrage – 'She's *my* guest!' – and dragged her in, over to the bar.

Esmé joined us, affronted because she hadn't been in the slightest challenged as to the exhibition of her orientation. Jackey must have been a bit pissed already because she laughed in her face.

Esmé shot me a wounded glance. She must have thought I had spilled the beans about the bisexual butterfly bit. There was nothing to be done but to get massively drunk.

Then, when Esmé went crawling around the crowd's periphery and did her performance-artiste-on-show dancing, I did spill the butterfly beans and Jackey laughed until she was sobbing into her beer.

'Michael's got his hands full there,' she said. 'Good. I hope she goes off and fucks some woman. It'll serve him right.'

'Hmm.'

'The trouble is, I can't help thinking we've got unfinished business, me and Michael.'

I couldn't say too much about this. My own business with him had been fairly surreptitious; an open and shut case swift as the slamming of a well-sprung closet door.

'We both invested so much in it. It was horrible. Two years of mental torture.'

'I remember.' I had been the one unloosening the thumb-screws, sawing holes in the iron maiden.

'We were Will and Anna Brangwen in *The Rainbow*. It was all pounding essences and eking out kernels and when it wasn't it was bloody boring. He's a manic depressive and she's welcome to him.'

'That's good to hear.'

We were having to shout over the noise of a remixed Doris Day. I didn't want Jackey to get emotional because she tended to cry quite easily and I'd never hear the out-pourings properly in that setting. I tried to change topics.

'Look at those clones lined up at the bar,' I said, unwisely pointing. 'They look like a rack of toothbrushes.'

She tried to smile. 'I still see them, you know.'

'What?'

'Those imaginary cows. From the acid trip in Michael's

home town. They come to haunt me, Paul, mooing and stamping their feet about my eating meat and walking out on Michael.'

'He threw you out!'

'I know, but – '

'He threw you out on a Sunday morning and made you hitch back to Leeds.'

'But betrayal is betrayal, whatever – '

'Oh, fuck betrayal! Look.'

On the dance floor Esmé had her tongue down some woman's throat. Jackey smiled bitterly. 'She's like Alien fucking Three. What does he see in her?'

I walked back with Esmé and Jackey on either arm. We went past a couple of nightclubs – *Thursdays is Ladies' Night! Free Nurses on Saturdays!* – past single men walking home alone, baffled by the sight of my two attendant handmaids. They weren't speaking; Esmé was being upset and disturbed by Jackey's silence, while Jackey was too drunk to care any more.

The bells gonged twice as we crossed the canal car park. Jackey extricated herself. 'I'll leave you before you go up that hill,' she said. 'I've got my key for Helen's house.' Tactfully she had elected to stay at the house of a different old friend. 'I'm off tomorrow. I'll be back to see you soon. Give me a hug.' We embraced with our usual vigour, the bizarre sexual chemistry blunted by alcohol.

Esmé made a big show of giving Jackey a no-hard-feelings-we-are-sisters hug. Jackey complied, although she might as well have been holding a lamppost. We watched her stagger off down a side road.

'All my friends make beautiful, filmic exits,' I said as we set off up the hill. 'It's one of my few demands; that when they leave, they do it beautifully.'

Esmé remained ominously quiet. Usually she would jump after a snippet like that like a kitten on a sock. Almost home she said, 'Jackey deserves to be happy. She's had it hard, too, hasn't she?'

I nodded. Esmé gave me a sickeningly consoling squeeze. 'It was such a shame it never worked out for her and Michael. But it wasn't right for them. Me and Michael are the right thing. He'll come to America in the end. But I hope Jackey finds someone soon. She needs to. You both do. You both deserve better. I just wish everyone was happy.'

By now we had reached our back door. I unlocked it and she inserted herself, exhausted, into the dark kitchen before I could. The air was heavy with the reek of stale spices.

I am dreaming, I think, about scarlet cows in bomber jackets. They crowd about me in moral indignation and I am dancing to ward them off, like Glenda Jackson in *Women in Love*.

Just past four in the morning I wake to the sound of screaming. A keening, babyish shriek. She's slashed her wrists, I think, propelling myself out of bed. On the landing there is Jack from upstairs, panic all over his face and belly hanging over his boxer shorts.

'She's screaming – go and see – Michael's just shot past me – on the stairs – He's run out of the house – '

As I race up the stairs the others are coming out of their rooms, dazed and frightened. How many people live here? Which room is Michael's?

The room that is smashed up; the light glaring on. The room is lifeless apart from Esmé sitting up in bed. She is rigid-backed, screaming, eyes like hardboiled eggs. Her wrists are held out; mercifully clean, harmless.

I grab her and she holds me hard, full of a sexless, destructive passion. She screams down my ear, a sound I have never heard so close in real life.

The rest of the house is congregating downstairs. Someone shouts that they are calling an ambulance. They imagine blood dripping from attic walls, sliding down the Schiele prints. Or the empty pill bottles, the slimy syringe. Her body is hard and yellow, naked and bony. Her jaw judders at my neck. Her screaming slows, is torn into ragged sobs. She heaves breath with difficulty.

'It's all right,' I intone, voice stunningly deep and clear. 'Esmé, Esmé, it's all right.'

She subsides; her nails loosen their grip on my T-shirt. She is calming down, slipping back into a lucid wakefulness.

'It was just a bad dream,' I tell her. 'Where's Michael?'

She works at her breathing.

'Easy, easy.'

I see everything clearly. She is pasty white. Her pupils are still rolled back. I look down and see my balls hanging negligently out of my shorts. We are complicit in an absurd intimacy. The drama is perfect.

Someone pops their head around the door, afraid.

'Michael's gone. He's ran away. The cunt!'

'Is the ambulance coming?'

'Jack went out to ring for one. What was it?'

I smoothed her back, urging her to breathe as I would do to a baby. 'I don't know if it was drugs or not. She can't talk. If it was, and the ambulance comes . . .'

He vanishes. I hear his steps thudding downstairs.

She gags on every word. 'I was drowning. I couldn't get up. Michael got frightened.'

'Calm down. Just calm down.'

She sucks up air in long gulps.

'Slower.'

'It's so sad, so sad,' she heaves. 'So sad.'

'Slower.'

'So sad!'

And she begins to pant again, faster and faster, and her eyes flip back like a doll's in their immaculate make-up. She stiffens in my arms. Something cracks and she stops breathing entirely.

'Esmé!'

For the first time I hear my own panic.

She starts to curl away from me, into a foetal shape. Something is ebbing out of her, or is it just the folding of her limbs away from me, her dull heaviness sinking back on the shabby duvet? She is silent.

And it was then I had to punch her, hard, to bring her back to life.

BARGAINS FOR CHARLOTTE

EACH STREET ON our estate of yellow box houses has a smaller box somewhere in it and these are bungalows for old people. They never look happy. In the street just down from us a car tore through the wall of their bungalow because it was right on the main road and they go mad on that corner. The car screamed through the itchyback bushes and bang: killed the old bloke inside on the spot. He'd been sitting watching daytime TV. Those walls must be held up with nothing.

Do the pensioners inside know the sort of danger they inhabit daily? Is their irksomeness excused by that knowledge of the threat of sudden, arbitrary demolishment?

Charlotte lives at the end of the row and she has nothing to complain about. Her bungalow is nowhere near the main road and her garden is smashing, nothing like the poky bits of concrete we've all got. You get all the perks if you're old. They put you on the phone for nothing. She had lovely flowers out all the year round, it seemed. She used to get a man in to do that, but now her garden arrangements have changed. Her garden is, if anything, even more sumptuous.

We always reckoned she must have quite a bit stashed away. Her husband had been someone, they said, and she still had an accent. Not posh but a bit southern, which marked her out. She played hell when the bairns went near her windows.

Think of a tortoise with white, flaccid skin and its shell crowbarred off. Charlotte to a T. You'd see her silhouetted in her french window of a night in her orthopaedic chair that swivelled round and we used to say that was her shell and she'd put herself back in for the night. She had one of those dowager's humps and we'd think it was wet and adhesive beneath her cardigan, fresh from the shell, lobster pink.

She never had tortoise hands – those are like elephants', aren't they? Though her fingers were oddly short, as if she'd worn them to the bone, working. Old, she still worked, in the Spastics Society shop down the precinct. Those short fingers had crossed my palm with copper once, when I was about ten – Hallowe'en 1980. We were running from door to door, wearing bin bags and asking for money. Charlotte made a big show of looking for her purse in all her kitchen drawers and asking me about my family. She seemed genuinely concerned about them, making me worry whether I wasn't concerned enough. Her questions placed them in peril, I felt. She hoped, she said, that my mummy and daddy would sort out their problems soon and that it wouldn't affect me too deeply.

Back home, later, I counted up my carrier of coppers and told my mam this in an offhand manner. She went up in a blue light. My dad and she were living in different places – he at one end of the estate and she, with us, at the other – on a social fiddle. The council had given him a single person's flat by the shop and the Chinky. We went over to hoover and dust every Saturday morning. His shared front door faced the grass at the back of the Chinky and I found heaps of discarded pink shrimps. For a while I thought they'd been *rained*, the way they said things got rained in *The Unexplained*, that magazine.

Mam said Charlotte was a nosy bitch.

Charlotte has worked down the Spastics shop for years. In there it always smells of washing powder and sweat. They arrange second-hand clothes on chrome stands in order of colour. In spring everything to the front of the shop is yellow. They fill the window with chickens made out of woolly pompoms. These are made by Charlotte, all winter long. Sits in her orthopaedic shell through the devastating cold days, when she lets the younger volunteer lasses do the earlier shifts, and she runs up furry lemon chickens. I bet it's a lonely thing being old on our estate. Even if they do put your phone line in free.

They're all pensioners who work in the Spastics shop down our town. Is this because they have more hours to fill in? When you are old, life has shrunk horribly to nothing and its warp and weft can't be pulled back to a decent size, no matter how much you tug. Surely in those circumstances you want to wring the best you can out of what's left? How can giving it all to charity constitute the best? An overflow, if anything, a by-product of pleasure: you can give leftovers to charity, but the main action?

I'd ask Charlotte if she was as selfless as this. Why does she put on that red nylon pinny in the morning to stand behind her counter doling out bargains, oddments, junk, other people's discarded crap?

Would she admit 'I get first dibs on the decent stuff'?

My goodness, the bargains!

The things people do away with!

They don't know when they're well off!

I tend to be in there quite often. I like to look at the books because they get quite a good, eclectic selection. There's always somebody literary dying in Aycliffe and their goodies wash up here. I became addicted to checking out the Spastics shop after finding *Anna Karenina* for fifty pence. But on every stiffened yellow page, can I inhale someone else's last gasp? It's a wonder if I can't. Intellectuals always smoke and these books are preserved with a laminate of nicotine. I think, Was this the book dropped from a dying grasp? This, the last sentence read? Look: I've read on further!

I'm educating myself to leave.

You really have to poke about, between Cartlands and Macleans, to find the good stuff. But it's there. *Jane Eyre* thirty pence.

I heard Charlotte speak quite sensitively to Ashley, a seven-foot-tall transsexual who models her hair on Liz Taylor in *Cleopatra*. She'd been hanging on to some special heels for her. They were a kind of present for after Ashley's op. I was in the day Charlotte produced them from under the counter;

but they were lime green. Ashley's face just dropped and he left the shop without buying anything at all. Charlotte was furious and took a perverse delight in telling the rest of the queue behind that the woman who'd just left had once been a man.

She collected handbags for one daft old wife, Sonja, who always wore a wig, though hers was for cancer, a beehive for ever on a tilt. Sonja said, 'It's forty-seven now! Forty-eight with this one, ta very much, Charlotte! And every one a different colour. I'd have a different bag to go with every outfit I could ever have!' Daft Sonja looked up at Charlotte again and Charlotte blinked those steady, judgemental eyes. 'Thank you, Charlotte. Would you keep a watch out for one in baby pink?'

Charlotte nodded tersely, regal arbiter of justice for cast-offs.

Expert, she sat each morning in the back room of the shop with her pot of tea and barrel of digestives (in the shape of Dougall, the dog from *The Magic Roundabout*) and for an hour or more she would go through the bags newly hauled in for redistribution. In the dusky half-light she would gut the plastic bin bags. They'd spill and strew like a trawler's nets. Turning stuff over in her hands, she'd inspect it, unfold and refold garments, giving them a good, careful sniffing. She counted the pieces in jigsaws and, in case one or two were missing, kept a spare, useless one to the side of her to make up the numbers. It all went with her job and her perk was first refusal and the chance to set a price on whatever she didn't care to offer the public.

She found an earthenware pot of gold coins. At first it looked like somebody's urn of ashes. Somebody, perhaps, whose treasured books were stacked in boxes close by. But the pot jangled inside and she heaved and grunted at the stuck lid until it popped free and the gold poured out on her lap.

'How much is here?' Charlotte cried, although she wasn't a greedy woman. She was careful and always had been. Her widow's pension went on the extravagant food she had delivered from Marks and Spencer of a weekend. Their white and green van pulled up beside her bungalow on Saturday mornings and Charlotte laid out a banquet for no one but herself. Seen in silhouette by the rest of our street. All of it would be out, uneaten, in the bottom of her wheely bin by Sunday morning. Sometimes we'd sneak a look: check. Miss Havisham. (*Great Expectations* forty-five pence.)

Her needs were met. They weren't always outrageous. But a whole pot of gold! Who'd turn their nose up at that?

'But what is it worth?' asked Charlotte of the bags and boxes of detritus, the heaps of semisoiled clothing, the single stuffed rocking donkey. 'What's the going rate for gold?'

And she saw, sitting astride the donkey, a human skeleton, bracing its frail weight on the felt saddle, gazing at her with terrible blank sockets. Its skull was disproportionately large. This was a baby's remains, rocking steadily on the donkey.

'I don't know what they give for gold,' said the child. 'These days.' Charlotte blinked, for now it was a fully fleshed child, chubby and brown, its head full of tangled curls. 'But think, Charlotte: if you bought this pot and took it home, wouldn't you lie awake and worry?'

She never worried. It was a point of honour with her. Her face clouded. 'Worry about what?'

'Even though your garden is wonderful, your bungalow is still ever so delicate. How easy for somebody to huff and puff and blow it in! How easy to take away your crock of gold! They leave rainbows behind, you know, for thieves to follow.'

Lips pursed, Charlotte was writing out a tiny label for the pot, '20p', and sticking it to the lid, which she had replaced. Really, it was an ugly thing. Ethnic-looking. No pattern on it or anything, no flowers. She shrugged, not to be put off.

'I'm not one of these silly old women who keep money and valuables vulnerable in the home and get murdered in their beds for it. My mattress isn't stuffed with fivers. I'd get these gold coins down to the bank at the first opportunity.'

The child had small wings flapping, but these were feather-less and thin: dead sycamore leaves. 'You might lose the gold coins on your way to the bank.' The child smiled. 'Wouldn't you fret that the gold shone through your pocket or your bag and everyone would know what you were carrying? Would you feel exposed?'

Charlotte was quick. She'd been a junior-school teacher once. She knew something about answering children back. 'Then I'd carry my gold in the urn. You can't see it shine through the urn, can you?'

She held up the nondescript pot in the meagre light of the room's flyblown lamp. The child squinted. 'I can,' he said. 'And what if the bank tricks you, gives you only half the gold's worth?'

'I can check the exchange rate,' said the old woman vaguely.

'Did you look at the coins? Aren't they strange and old? Perhaps, for all they may look like gold, they are useless here and now? Mightn't they excite suspicion and cause the bank people to point their fingers at you and jab at their alarm buttons?'

Charlotte had heard enough. She left the storeroom clutching her new pot and paid for it down in the shop, wrapping it and putting it away in her bag before anyone could inspect it.

But that night she walked home nervously across the Burn. She imagined that every stranger she passed could see through her shopping bag and knew about her treasure.

The next day was Saturday; there was no going to the bank. She had her usual banquet and the only person she saw all day was the cheery delivery boy from Marksies in his green and white van. He came up the garden path with her usual boxes of luxury items. Charlotte startled him this time with a tip. He careered off in the van a little wildly, she thought, dangerously.

She sat down to her feast with a heavy heart. The pot was in pride of place like a centrepiece at Christmas dinner, surrounded by cakes and dips and asparagus tips, flans and chicken drumsticks and salads busy with colour, stiff with dressings. The urn of gold seemed to exert its own dull pressure on her spirits. 'Get rid of me,' it urged tonelessly; 'I'll bring you nothing but ill fortune. Why didn't my last owner cash me in? Have you thought about that?'

'That's a point,' the infant clucked, fleshly again and sitting across the table from Charlotte. 'One simply doesn't get lucky like this. Gold coins! It doesn't happen! Not to people like us!'

'Why are you going on at me like this? What do you want?' She was a touch distraught.

The child looked solemn. 'Allow me to do your garden. I'd like that.'

Overcome, Charlotte stood shakily and went to embrace the child, but she tripped on the rug beneath the table, fell and hit her head.

She came to, feeling dreadful, quite early on Sunday morning. With a throbbing headache she emptied the ruined party food into her wheely bin. While out there she took in her garden. It was looking unkempt by now. Her little man hadn't been round in a while.

She went to bed for the rest of the day, leaving Classic FM playing on the Teasmade by her bed. She mulled over the course her life was taking.

All Sunday she dreamed listlessly of when she was married to a soldier and taught children and had a garden with roses in the south.

Monday morning she was late in at the Spastics shop. She'd stopped down the Burn on her way and, in a little ceremony on the wooden bridge, dropped the pot in the water. It hit with a ker-plunk. The water looked exactly like morning sun coming through her full cafetiere. She went to work.

Monday morning meant a good deal of new belongings in the back room. Charlotte put on her rubber gloves. This Monday was a little below par, she thought. Or maybe she was disgruntled, throwing a fortune away. She almost wished she was religious; couldn't she have felt virtuous, performing a sacrifice like that?

She struggled with the clasp of a battered blue suitcase. Picturing the gold scattered on the rocks in the Burn. Those stunted fish nosing at the abandoned coins. There was definitely something inside the case; she had to check.

Not many books this week. Not many bargains for me, she was afraid. (Though she was wrong, I found. *Lady Chatterley* twenty pence. But it was my own copy, donated out of spite by my sister.) And inside the case: heaps of crumbling newspaper. It came onto her fingers like grey pollen and went up her nose. The pages were dated 1933 and a heavy stench came out after all that time: rotten fish and chips. The papers were bundled around some light, solid object and she worked into this parcel, soon discovering the child's skeleton.

Silhouetted that evening in the matte blue window of her yellow brick of a bungalow we could see Charlotte slumped in her swivelling tortoise shell. She watched, rapt, while the child sat up at the smallest of her nest of tables and ravenously ate a meal she had cooked him. His bones were faintly yellowed, slick with plaque.

At last the child finished his first supper for many years, belched, and began:

'I was a child who menaced an old man who lived down our lane. He worked in his garden and I would stand in his gateway, aping his every action in order to annoy him. Cutting grass, pruning hedges, pressing saplings into the earth. I'd take him off for badness' sake. I was only a child. Only learning. And one day he must have had enough because he brought out a sharp knife and I thought, This is it! I've pushed my luck!

'Yet he came nowhere near me. He simply mimed, for my benefit, slashing his own throat, there and then in his garden. Then he went in for his tea, still furious, leaving the knife on the lawn.

'When he returned for a last go at his beds, there he found me, white and slashed in a gleaming pool on his garden path.'

'There, there,' Charlotte consoled him.

An emaciated cupid, a stripeless buzzing bumblebee has supplanted Charlotte's young man in the garden. You can see the skeletal child hovering about her shrubs in the very middle of the night, if you're coming in late, sneaking round the houses. The child will have secateurs in hand, being businesslike, wearing its ineluctable maniac's grin. But the child is glad of the work. He's handy, too, because his spiritual powers and know-how ward off disasters. So Charlotte hopes she'll never get a van or a lorry through her front-room wall, like that old bloke did. She exists within an enchanted circle of the child's deceit and sups contentedly alone still, on Saturday nights.

COLD COMPANIONABLE STREAMS

'LOOK!'

My mother, Hilde, pointed out to sea. We were walking across the scrubby headland. It was a treat; the place I used to walk with Father. In this evening's lowering gloom, however, we found there was no more enjoyment to be squeezed from this place. Things had changed.

'Eliza, look!'

She dug me in the ribs, and I was forced – rather sulkily; I was, with good reason, I think, an uncommunicative adolescent – to glance across the bay. The sun was setting; sky, land and water had acquiesced to the colour and texture of raw, streaky bacon. Eleven wild swans ruffled this calm.

'Eleven!' Hilde sighed. I shall call her Hilde; she was never my real mother.

'So?'

Her face twisted itself into one of those pitying leers. My slow-wittedness was, she claimed, the bane of her life. Already it had caused me endless trouble. Surely even I ought to see the prudence in learning to think for myself?

'So?' I stubbornly reiterated.

'Where there is eleven, or any odd number, there will dissatisfaction be,' she pronounced with infinite patience and just a hint of martyrdom. She was, you will remember, the most famous widow in the land. 'One of that number is doomed to have no mate. Which do you suppose it is?'

This was a test of my burgeoning maturity and wisdom, I felt sure. Some ominous decision pended on my reply. I was used to the entire armoury of Damocles suspended above my

164

head, every moment of the day. Hilde liked to set intellectual traps for me, with the penance of my being sent away if I failed them. Traps and testings were sprung from every niche of the domestic environment: What does one do with spilt sugar? Where does the Spirit of the Hearth sleep? It was all very wearing.

I stared at the swans gliding seemingly purposelessly in a neat V formation. They seemed to be identical. 'I have no idea,' I breathed, giving myself up to her scorn.

'Quite right,' she murmured, shielding her eyes as she gazed at their spectacle. 'Dissatisfaction is a difficult thing to locate at first glance. You were wise not to hazard a guess. I suggest you stay here until dawn before you divine your true opinion of which of the eleven is the – shall we say – odd one out. I'm heading home for a rendezvous with the archbishop and will send him in the car for you tomorrow at dawn. If your answer does not tally with mine, I shall have you sent to St Tuoni's School for Errant Girls, and you will not be allowed to return to your dear departed father's house until, at least, my death. Good night, my dear.'

Stunned, I watched her traipse her soggy way back across the colour-bleached headland. Then I found a rock and sat on it as the horizon's curtains began to gather in darkening folds, the light hushing into anonymity like a theatre audience as the performance seems ready to begin. And I watched the eleven swans still circling the bay.

In Australia it was once believed that the black swans had been people. People who, when menaced by flood, learned to grow feathers – and extra long, supple necks, presumably to enable them to see round the future's corner for further natural disasters.

But people become swans for all sorts of reasons. The Valkyries disguised themselves – oh, dear, this is complicated – as swan-maidens; that is, women who had turned themselves into swans, in order to enable the warriors whose military successes they had invisibly controlled while up in the ether, to fall in love with them. A lovely display of wiles and power, I think: the Valkyrie laying down her wings by the poolside while she bathes, allowing the warrior to think he has come upon her by chance. Perhaps the masochistic dear thinks he has found another Diana; anticipates being torn to shreds by her hounds. But she has led him, as she led him unwittingly into battle, to fall at her feet and believe he has the upper hand simply because he has possession of her wings – her false wings. The Valkyrie's wings are optional accessories.

So it was these thoughts I turned over, with the water-smoothed pebbles between my toes, sitting among the reeds on the bank. I admit I entertained the odd Leda-inspired fantasy. What if the dissatisfied swan, the 'odd one out', popped down earthwards, brought his brute-blood to bear upon . . . But I was getting too old for that kind of speculation. Violation fantasies held none of the appeal that they might have in my earlier, politically less informed days. Looking back, I really don't know what I had been dreaming about. But, like the Valkyrie's wings, none of our dreams are natural, are they? They are accessories bought for us by other hands, stocking fillers that we have to walk around with in the waking dream of our lives. And we wonder why we feel foot-bound, why we hobble, when we wear these Christmas stockings and think them roller-skates.

My brothers, before they went, supplied me with all sorts of impedimenta. Impedimenta for the feet . . . high-heeled shoes, my mother's, my 'real' mother's shoes, which were left in the cupboard underneath the marble staircase. Red stilettos fished out of the drab garbage one day by my youngest brother. My brothers tortured me, I think it fair to say. Yes, there were eleven of them, and in their attic room I stood in the centre of the gapless circle they made and I had to parade naked in those shoes.

Their impedimenta were mental accoutrements, the bric-a-brac of their fantasies that hindered our waking lives in our chilly, motherless home like overfilled backpacks hamper an army's progress.

I had an army of brothers, an alert rank of male peers,

their bodies and faces seemingly identical, impersonal, intent on merely the violation of myself. I was the other, I was the strange one. When they stood in their circle, who defied their difference with her very different being?

And downstairs paced my stepmother Hilde, holding at bay our father, who in turn believed himself master of her. He thought he had her Valkyrie wings locked in the armoury. But he didn't. She held the keys; especially the keys to the attic where, one by one, my brothers stretched across and pestled sputum and spunk into me.

But I was merely the cabaret; a diversion. I was the healthy reclamation of their appetites; my gender symbolised the recuperation of their heterosexuality for, when I was lifeless, limp, a tattered rag that bled and disgusted them on that wooden floor the colour of gruyere cheese . . . they would return to the task in hand and fuck each other, as one swift and efficient body of men.

When the sun came down and it was almost dark, the swans alighted on the beach, a little distance from me. And, indeed, they shed their feathers, for at night my stepmother's magic could hold no sway over them. In a heap of white pillow stuffings my eleven brothers looked exhausted and relieved. They clasped each other and gazed at their sun-reddened bodies. I still felt a certain fondness, I must admit. From where I sat, fingers clenching pebbles in shock, they looked quite harmless. They were thin with tiredness and a diet of fish, their hair was lank and long and their inert genitalia useless and pale as the eyes of potatoes. I stood up and waved to them.

One by one my brothers embraced me. Their flesh was rubbery, worn lifeless in the wind. The youngest explained that, cursed as they were, they must fly all day in the shape of swans, in the face of the sun, and never set their feet on earth or water. When night came, since they reverted so swiftly, they must find land – or fall, like Icarus, in a shower of useless feathers.

We sat on the shore, softened and white in the moonlight,

in silence for a while. Their plumage, all around us, was warm and fluffed out with air. It looked very much as if we were in the wreckage of their attic room, in pleasanter, more innocent times, after an enthusiastic pillow fight.

But there never were innocent times. Now, as then, my brothers were animals. They were pornographers of the vilest kind; desire had no context for them. It was a *raison d'être*, having nothing to do with identity. The pillow fights then would end as this feather shower was now ending: two or three were ignoring my presence entirely, were sprawled upon the bracken, one slipping another a length of his grubby cock, happy to be human again.

My youngest brother talked me through the night.

'We do not usually come here. Today has been an unusual day, to return so close to our place of origin. We rest at night, in human form, on a little rock in the sea, far from here. We must huddle together. If the sea is rough, the foam spurts over us, but we cling on for dear life.'

'Why did you come back here?' I asked.

'Twice a year are the days long enough for us to fly as far as this place. We come to see you, Eliza. We watch over you, and then we return to our rock.'

My guardian angels! Gabriels all, though you would hardly credit it. Most of them seemed vastly unimpressed by the business of the night, fingering and pulling at each other in the most desultory fashion.

'We have been wrongly punished, our sister. You must break this spell.'

I let this settle in, implications coaxing their way through the deceptive silence. The surf's gloating throb and boom, the grunting of the lovers on the freckled shore. I let him stew for a while. I owed them nothing.

But before dawn came I realised that I had no answer for Hilde. Which was the odd one out? There was no way of telling. The boys were set out like a debauched football team, smeared in each other's juices. The youngest had left me still deciding whether to help their cause, while he submitted to a swift and surly fuck from another whose name, I am pleased to relate, I had forgotten. But they left me alone. Obviously they needed me.

So it was because I was none the wiser that I went with them. That morning, as the sunlight eased into the gloom and their silhouettes were broken up, smoothed out in its casual wash, I told them I would come with them to their rock in the sea for that day. Their torsos constricted, became round and pregnant bird breasts, their sculpted necks stretching painfully into white serpents. They howled as their faces were broken off into stubby beaks, their feet splayed into clumsy webs, their cocks reared up into their bodies. My brothers made a raft of their wings and closed about me in tight formation, carrying me surely into morning.

Justice? I'm not so sure what it is. When Valkyries succeeded in getting a chosen warrior to fall in love with them, there were always problems. They weren't blind, those girls. Why, by the watersides as they were doing their fan dances with assumed swan's wings and enticing old Ethelred or whoever, they were always aware of a certain niggling doubt. Odin would bring them to justice for attempting to articulate their desires. It isn't fair, none of it is fair. Is Ethelred or whoever punished? No, but neither is he fairly exercising his desires. He has been hoodwinked by the feathered Salome from the skies. Odin was, in those cases, absolute. His not so tender mercies came like the thunderbolts that shattered the poor and virtuous Justine in de Sade's tale. As I grow older I wonder about de Sade; was he such a monster after all? He opposed, with every perverted fibre of his being, the likes of Odin. It was on Odin's instructions that the Valkyries would alter the course of great battles. Unseen they would stab, slaughter and whisper in the ears of their victims. But if a Valkyrie fell for a member of the away team, the team that Odin had decreed must fall . . . well, then there was a ruckus. Justice, you see, is a moot point. Who am I to say what my brothers deserved? Or Hilde for that matter. All I can relate, and not wholly impartially, is what they got.

*　　*　　*

We flew all day across the limitless seas. The land slipped away behind us, and I could hardly credit my earlier fear at being sent away to a school for bad girls. What fear could hold me now, aloft?

They were flying slowly, much more slowly than usual, as my youngest brother informed me. I was weighing them down and already, as we entered the latter half of the afternoon, there were mutinous squawkings in the squadron's hindquarters; 'We aren't going to make it before nightfall. She's brought us disaster.'

Curiously, I felt only the mildest of perturbations at this. Indeed, it was somewhat satisfying to be regarded as the albatross, hung irrevocably around my errant brothers' necks.

I spent the day watching the waters below, strung out in leisure on my feathery hammock. As I say, people have become swans for all sorts of reasons. The Australians, in the arid outback, were terrified of flooding. They twisted themselves into the malevolent black swan, like those that haunt the underworld's tepid rivers in Finnish mythology. The water determined their form as it does the gnarling of cliff edges, the gentle convexity of pebbles. Softly as an irreversible spell the tide creeps in and out under the moon's stark guidance.

My stepmother, too, had set her spell in silence. We wondered why she haunted graveyards for nettles, pulped, mashed, spun and wove them into eleven fine green shirts. Then we discovered she was after revenge for my violation. It was for me that she presented my brothers with the shirts. Changed utterly, my brothers took flight.

I think they secretly knew I could be of no help to them. But they hoped, they hoped. I simply wanted to tell them, Make the best of it. Aren't you happy as swans? Sufficient unto yourselves, your own closed circuit of desire, swooping by day over the multitudinous cross-currents that everywhere determine the form and shape of lives? At least you are now immutable, you swans. Violence is a reaction to the fear and apprehension one experiences in the face of mutability. You are freed of violence; set in your ways as you are, inviolable and muted, mute swans. Is that not enough?

But no. They wished to be 'human' again, they wanted my help still, and I was not to withhold it.

I never even had to try to exact justice. Odin, or whoever, saw to it for me. Gravity it was, I rather think, that exerted its influence, and declared that there would be no leniency for them.

As daylight waned, the sanctuary of their rock was nowhere in sight. The oldest brother, he who had first been transformed, reverted first to human form. He fell, and in shocked, panicked silence, the others beat on into the gathering night. Then another, and another. The remaining brothers shouldered their increasing responsibility for my mass and pushed desperately onwards, upwards, hoping for land. Another, another. They slipped out from under us with barely a scream. Those left were breathing ragged the length of their tortured, elegant necks. Flecks of blood and spittle appeared on their beaks. More, more of them fell.

Still I was not frightened.

The flight slowed down. We would never make it. We realised now.

Soon I was wrestling in mid-air with my youngest brother. He was the last one left and, as I discovered, utterly useless. One of his wings was still a human arm, just as, when human, one arm was a wing. His brothers had been buoying him up. His was the nettle shirt with the left arm incomplete.

'I am the odd one out.' He smiled ruefully, as he ruptured in flight and spread out bare-limbed. Human-formed, yet with one comically inept, immaculate bird's wing, he dropped into the ocean below.

And I? I flew away.

I had my answer now, with which to confront Hilde. I had also discovered my vocation in life. And with that, I might do anything. Hilde was reduced to piddling about with archbishops and princes. Now that I had shed my feathery impedimenta, I pretty much had the world at my feet.

WILL YOU STAY IN OUR
LOVERS' STORY?

SHE HATED HIM first of all because he had silver hair. Her mother was stroking it the first time Mandy clapped eyes on him.

'This is your new dad,' her mother said, sitting next to him on the kitchen bench.

'But he's old,' Mandy said and they laughed. When she remembered her first dad, he was young. He was up to his knees in the river, catching sticklebacks for her, and his face was prickled softly with beard.

Now Mam and this Les were laughing and getting married. His eyes creased up and closed in when he laughed. She hoped he would never come to pick her up from school.

The registry office smelled of disinfectant and new flowers. Outside the room where Mam and Les married each other, there was a large board full of names. Each name had a number beside it. Mandy, in her crinkled new green dress, read them all while they waited to go in. 'They're all old,' she thought. Her head swam. Then Mam, shaking with nerves, ushered her in.

Two old women did the service. There wasn't a vicar. Everything was silver and blue, even the flowers. The fat woman read the words out, Mam and Les repeated them. A thinner woman at a desk nearby was writing in a big yellow book. She blew on the page when she finished, as if the ink was hot.

'Isn't this a nice family group?' the thinner woman sighed,

taking their photo when it was all over. 'I hope I don't cut your heads off.'

She gave Mandy a special smile.

Les sprawled. He made a mess of their house, although Mam didn't seem to mind. Mandy watched him make a pot of tea to watch telly with. He left tea bags steaming in the sink and clogging the plughole. The bench was sticky with wet sugar. He ate chocolate biscuits, humming through the crumbs as he poured out. Mam sat with the telly, not minding.

It was Les's idea to cut down on fuel bills. He had read something in the Sunday paper, he said, about saving electricity.

'Sounds like a good idea,' said Mam and switched off the heating. All three curled up on the settee to watch the telly, a duvet over their knees, pulled up to their chins. Mandy had to sit between them all night. She couldn't get out, even when she got bored. Les ate crisps. She listened to him mashing them to a slimy pulp.

When there was a film on he fell asleep next to her. Old people did that. He never saw the end of a film. She heard the breath startle in his throat, listened to the slight, fluting snores from his nose. His head would touch down on her shoulder, as if he were comfortable with her. For the rest of the film she would have his bristly silver hair weighing down on her.

And he wasn't comfortable with her. When they took Mam to the doctor's and neither of them was allowed to go in with her, they would have to sit together in the waiting room. He kept quiet. He couldn't think of anything to say. Yet, when her mam was there, he would be coming out with all sorts of things.

'Do you know what windmills are for, Mandy?'

'What are you reading at school, Mand?'

'What do you think Mummy would like for her birthday?'

He called Mam Mummy. Mandy never called her that. She didn't even look like a mummy.

He gave a sigh of relief when Mam came out of the consulting room. Not because she was smiling, the doctor hadn't given her bad news, but because Mummy was there again, between them. It was easier with three of them there.

Mandy liked it best when it was just her and Mam. It was like old times when they went to the shops together. Mandy wasn't old enough to call this nostalgia. They would sit in a café and Mandy would get a plate of chips. Mam would pinch one, letting it cool for a moment on her saucer.

'You could talk to Les more.'

'I do talk to him.' She could feel her socks slipping off. When Mam asked questions like this, Mandy imagined that a small vicious dog under the table was tugging her shoes and then her socks off for spite. She had to pretend nothing was happening.

'You grunt at him. He's only trying to be nice.'

'He asks stupid things.'

'Pardon, madam?'

'I'll try.'

It was on one of these trips that Mam took bad. Mandy hated Les even more for not being there with his car. It ended up with Mandy calling for her first taxi.

They were pushing a trolley between them through the supermarket's automatic doors. They had a lot to get. Mam waved a long list about, then clasped her head. She grabbed her bag off the trolley.

'Mam?'

Mam whirled round and ran back out of the double doors.

The duvet went back upstairs. Mam under it, in bed. The heating went back on. Mandy watched the telly with Les and he watched *The Benny Hill Show*. He laughed all the way through. His short, barking laugh filled the room. Mandy couldn't see what he was laughing at. She tried her best to join in and even talk to him.

'When will Mam be better?'

174

He stopped mid-laugh and looked at her, mouth hanging open, full of crisps.

Les started taking Mandy to and from school. He waited outside with all the mams and seemed pleased to see her. He stood a little apart from the others and they didn't try to include him. A few asked how Mandy's mam was and Les was rude to them.

'She's all right,' he said, tight-lipped. Mandy blushed with shame.

'They're Mam's friends,' she said as they walked off quickly, quicker than everyone else.

'Your mam doesn't need friends. She's got me.'

It got to the summer holidays. Mam's room was hot, musty, dark green. Her bedside table was covered with bottles of pills, cups half-empty with soured barley water and scummed coffee. Les was reading to her in a loud, clear voice, Catherine Cookson novels, one after another. He didn't try to put any life into the voices, but Mam seemed to be asleep most of the time anyway.

One morning Les woke Mandy up.

'Get up, Mand. We're going on a trip.'

He opened her curtains. Mandy screwed up her eyes.

'Where to?'

His hair was white in the light. 'Flamingoland. Get dressed.'

Now that Les was here they were supposed to have holidays. More money now, Mam had said. Two weeks away in a caravan. Coniston maybe. Pack up his car and ride away over the hills. Picnics, plodging, going round shops. Les had said they would go mad with all his money. It was useless until he had met Mandy's mam. He would *lavish* it on them, he said. Their lives would change for ever. First, though, Mam had to stop the tranquillisers.

She was trying hard. Failing. Trying harder. But she couldn't go on holiday yet. She explained to Mandy that she wanted to be taken back home to her sickbed each night. 'So it'll be day trips we'll be having this summer,' she said. Scarborough, Ullswater, Flamingoland.

She got a letter from the TV people one morning and Les had to write back for her. She couldn't take her place on the team for *Family Fortunes* because she was bad.

'There,' Les spat as he wrote. 'That's what them tablets are doing to you. You can't go on the telly stoned to the eyeballs.'

Mandy was watching her mam, lying on the settee. Her eyes were like Cleopatra's in history books, but she wasn't wearing make-up.

Aunty Christine, who was clever and would have gone to college if it wasn't for that insurance clerk, took Mam's place on *Family Fortunes*. Grandma was disappointed in her. She thought she might have pulled herself together in time. But she didn't come to visit. Their family team won three thousand pounds.

Mam, Les and Mandy watched it from under the duvet. Mam came down for the evening for once, even though she already knew how it ended. Grandma and her sisters had already blown the money on a holiday. Mam thought her sisters looked tarty. They were abroad now.

'All the questions were easy,' said Mam afterwards as her family waved to her under the rolling credits. 'I'd have won that.'

'We know, love,' Les said.

Mandy went looking for clothes in the washing basket, wondering what was suitable for Flamingoland Zoo.

Last night Les had said, 'Mandy . . .' He looked around him as if he thought someone might be listening. 'One day soon, your mummy might well die.'

Dungarees, she thought. It's bound to be muddy.

Mam was walking slowly. She was withdrawing again. Les put his arm around her waist and helped her along. Mandy watched them, sitting in the passenger seat of Les's car. He had parked at the edge of a brown lake. She didn't want to see the flamingos, but Mam did. Les was practically pulling her to the edge of the water. Mandy put the radio on.

They had already driven through the bits with the lions

and the rhinos running wild. It wasn't very scary because they all looked tired.

Mandy didn't want to watch. Les holding Mam up on the gravelly shore, pointing at the big pink turkeys on their spindly legs. The birds waded awkwardly, shot into and out of the air, skimmed over the calm surface. Mam was craning her neck about to see. Mandy watched.

Les had left the keys in the ignition. They swung there and Mandy wished she could drive. She locked the car doors and rolled the windows up. The radio got on her nerves so she switched it off and listened to herself breathe. She misted up the windscreen and wiped it away with her cardigan sleeve, misted it again.

Two men had appeared and were talking to Mam and Les. Mandy frowned because they seemed to be arguing. I bet we're not supposed to park here, she thought. Then she saw that the men had silver hair like Les, and folded wings hanging out of the back of their dresses. They took Mam's arms and held her between them. Mam looked wildly about her and Mandy could hear Les shouting, even with the windows rolled up. He was throwing a tantrum, as the great white wings began to beat.

And then Mam seemed to calm down. The men with wings were digging into the pockets of their frocks and producing handfuls of sweets; Smarties, M and M's. They pushed them into Mam's face and she swallowed and seemed to sag between them. Mam's sandalled feet left the beach's shingle.

Les came running back to the car. He tried to open the door. But Mandy had locked it.

'Mand! Open this door!' he yelled, pulling at the handle. He wanted to drag Mam back into the car, whisk them back home, shove her back under the duvet and read her Catherine Cookson.

'Mand! Mandy!'

Mandy wiped the rest of the fog from the window. Mam had been lifted right off the ground and she was struggling only slightly now. The angels had stopped feeding her and they let the Smarties drop in a fine rainbow shower beneath them. It drummed and rattled on the car roof for a while. Mandy saw multicoloured capsules bouncing off the bonnet, off Les's coat, sticking in his silvery hair. Then the shower finished.

The flamingos, who had raised their horned beaks to watch the flight, looked back at the water now that the show was finished and dredged the lake bottom for sweets.

COULD IT BE MAGIC?

I KEPT ON at you with a fierce, perverse love, didn't I?

Things like this were the reason.

We sat somewhere public, bottle of yellow wine between us – you were getting me into wine and I admitted preferring being pissed on wine to being pissed on lager – and you started fingering the petals of the silk freesias they'd stuck in a mineral-water bottle.

They were so purple and realistic-looking, I waited to see pollen smudging your skin.

You said you loathed silk flowers. That loud, admonishing tone you'd take on often in my presence. Never about me, but about things close to me. The accoutrements to our little scenes.

I asked why you hated them.

'Because they aren't plastic flowers.'

This morning I'm back in my own town. Far from your presence and your influence.

'Out from under that man's skin,' came a postcard from Vienna, from my mother, in the post this morning. Nothing from you, urging me back to our flat. She thinks I'm well shot of you. She never liked you and she's dying to return from singing in Vienna to see how her darling son's getting on by himself. She asks in her postcard if I've signed myself up with the doctors here.

I had an appointment straight away. They've had it all done up and Dr Jones's office is a cosy orange. An atmosphere of slightly overdone toast which lulls you (well, me, at any rate), and he had me up on the bench starkers in minutes giving me the once-over. Those cool utensils.

We talked about depression. Pills will sap me and he says he's loath to do that just yet. Shit. So I'm thrown back on my own resources and he clapped his fat hands with glee to hear me resolve that I would somehow pull my own self together. He asked about you and I said there'd be no counting on you.

'Have you ever thought of doing harm to yourself?' he asked solemnly and I almost laughed. The cleaner nosed in to empty his bins. Crumpled yellow papers and dead syringes. He looked at me expectantly while she fussed on.

All I could say was, 'No more than any other incipient artist and homosexual living in Newton Aycliffe.'

So we closed with a chuckle and he promised to see me soon.

I still didn't have any proper answers. I went straight to the gym to work off my frustrations. There I take special advice about how much iron I ought to be pumping. In my condition. I don't want to hurt the baby.

Your smart flat – which you encouraged me to think of as our smart flat – was crammed with plastic flowers.

In this house I have real flowers. Here I wait for the opera queen back from the continent, periodically dusting the furniture's blank patches which I can feel ache for Venetian glass. Do I hear the chinking and chiming of approaching maternal baggage?

You had pink tulips and ice-blue arum lilies. I can see you even now picking up the lot, stem by stem, stomping from vase to vase, then dumping them all in the kitchen sink, giving them a good slosh of washing-up liquid.

When you were pissed off with me you'd give the flowers a scrubbing. It was your way.

In this house there is no tension. Nothing like the sexual atmospherics we'd practise without realising. I need to put my feet up.

In your smart flat by the acid-green lilies you'd pounce

on me from nowhere and fuck me on the carpet. You had your little ways and the physical advantage over me. Once the storm was broken, though, you could turn tender and I see now, when I think back, those hands of yours, cupped like petals about my cock's stamen. I can't think about this now. I'm home.

'Plastic flowers know exactly what they are. They aren't very realistic and they *know* that. They don't pretend to be anything different. They're proud of being bogus.'

To me that sounded well thought out and impressive. I determined to argue the opposite because that's what you liked. You didn't want a toadying lapdog who *agreed*. You wanted me with a mind of my own. Right.

'I like silk flowers best.'

You raised that eyebrow, the one that waits, hell-bent on explication.

'Plastic flowers remind me of visiting my aunties in the seventies, when I was a kid. Everything was overcolourful but dusty and tawdry.'

'Uh-oh,' you said. 'Generation gap opening up.'

'But it's true!' I burst out, getting interested now. 'I'm attracted to the silk flowers out of pathos. They're not real and they know they don't look *quite* real – being too regular and a touch too pastel – but they're making a pathetic and ultimately doomed show at authenticity.'

Your head was shaking. '*How* eighties!'

I wasn't going to argue. 'That's what I am, aren't I?'

'And I'm seventies.'

'Right.'

'And that's some justification for your god-awful taste?'

'Actually – ' and here I grinned – 'I'm a nineties person and so I like real flowers.'

'Oh, fuck off!' It was quite a shock to hear you swear. You never swore much; it was me who was common. You had massive coffee cups and Cocteau-engraved ashtrays and didn't even smoke. 'You can't have that. Real flowers don't come into it.'

These were the things we talked about. And it was fun, wasn't it? Exploring our relative states. Never blinding ourselves about each other. Early on you said, 'Vive la différence.' Even in a same-sex do, you said, there needed to be polarities at work. That was why you liked younger men. My opinions were unconfirmed; I'd just drifted.

You thought I was a simple narcissist who wanted someone even younger than me. I was your best fantasy. My body was the house of all our desires, it seemed for a time. Well, now.

'Surely you're everyone's perfect idea of St Sebastian?'

Sometimes you'd say things that would put me off, like the above.

Do you think this is funny? About sea horses, the male of the species. You once said – because we were fond of marine life at one stage, weren't we? – that they looked as much like ears as horses.

The shape and curl of the things. Sea-ear-horse.

We found it was the male who gave birth. When we went to underwater zoos we watched, rapt whole Saturdays, through plate glass. The males, with those gorgeous unblinking blue eyes, slunk off behind the pond weed and then . . . Well, they had these inflated chests, puffed up proudly, and there was a dilating hole at the top and he would nod his snout to some sure, internal tune, waiting . . . and then (there really should be suitable musical accompaniment) out popped *millions* of tiny sea-horse babies, perfectly formed, swirling about in billows like roped silk hankies being yanked from the horse's belly. It was beautiful, we thought.

And marmosets and siamangs and arrow-poison frogs and jaçanas and damsel fishes and mouth-breeding bettas and rheas and mallee fowl and phalaropes. See? We're all at it.

Don't you think that's funny?

My town is a grim town. You always said that and it's the one place you will never follow me to. With my mother in Vienna and you scared of the grim north, I have a few weeks' reprieve. Time to work out, sit in cafés all day long, gestating quietly.

You used to slink past this town on Intercity as you used to slink past the whole of the north. We lived in our London flat and commuted to Scotland where you'd teach, desultorily. The north was Intercity's nastiest interlude. When I travelled with you I'd gaze across the north's fields of rape, thinking about before I knew you.

But in my grim town I've found a café even you wouldn't sniff at. The coffee comes in massive cups and saucers – continental Alice in Wonderland cups, bright yellow – and the waiter is South African and on warm days wears a kilt. In the mornings he brings me Greek yoghurt with fruit, which I crave now, as he helps me up the stairs to my usual table. I need help now, with all my swellings. I'm training less at the gym as my day arrives. For a little while it made an improvement. In the gym I hardened up, from Donatello's to Michelangelo's David. You always said men could be divided into those who preferred one or the other. Now I'm neither and ripe and the beautiful man in a kilt struggles to help me up to the café.

I can sit, abstractedly, and I know people wonder why I sit so long and why I look . . . well, expectant.

Is the waiter in a kilt younger than me? He says he left the army, ran a bar in Greece three years before coming here. So maybe he's older. I wonder, is he fit to look after my children?

Jazz plays; the whitewashed walls show selected paintings from a nearby school. I'm fond of the place. It's a bit of your precious continent beside Newton Aycliffe.

On those train rides where you'd duck your head from the north, we'd sit opposite each other and on the table there'd be your *Guardian*, my *Smash Hits*. Would people ever believe we were together? You'd fall asleep in your teaching outfit, head lolled back.

Did I tell you about the young bloke who took the place next to you, who sneered at your snoring and smirked my way, allying us against your complacent, momentary repulsiveness? Did I betray you in that moment? Did the cock crow?

He fell asleep himself, just out of York. He wore an old purple tracksuit, full of little bobbles from the wash. There was late-afternoon sun, trapping the air like marmalade in the carriage, making sweat stand on us, slick as confidence.

I watched you both snooze and the bloke in the purple tracksuit got himself a slow, elegant horn on. The thick cotton of his tracksuit caricatured the shape of him and, fascinated, I watched him pulse with the train's rocking.

Before he shocked himself awake, he drew a lazy hand down to cover it with a touchingly public caress. He was a pretty young bloke; saw me watching when he woke, didn't mind. He got off a little later.

You slept still and I thought about you, white, and the stale smell of you underneath. A kind of brie and decades' worth of smoke ground up in your pores. Your body, its smell; how inscrutable it all was to me. I could tell the other bloke a mile off, read him plainly as I could that fabulous cock of his. There was no real need for me to follow him off the train. Though I was tempted. And did I really get fucked off him in the train's bog? Would I tell you? Is this kid – horror of horrors – his? Are you set on being a dad?

Vive la différence, you said, justifying your love for Donatello's more boyish David. I use the same to praise your older body. Your flesh hangs heavier and your gestures of privacy are touching in ways youth's public shows can be. I love you for when you woke on that train and said you had to go to the loo and, too polite to say loo aloud, you nodded in its direction. Was it the same loo I had conceived our child in, minutes before?

'Fabulous kilt,' I pluck up and say when he brings my coffee.

'Uh . . .' he begins, and elects to play it safe. 'It's just right for this weather.'

For today the grim town steams, below the wide wooden blinds of the café. It could be stifling to be anywhere other than here. I'm flicking through Maugham's *Summing Up* and it's portentous, deeply miserable under all the epiphanies. Maugham reminds me – forgive me – a bit of you. Loves the sound of his own epiphanies.

I want to hear this waiter talk.

'Uh . . . you're really engrossed then?' he says.

I thought he meant with the child!

'Good book?'

'Not really.'

'Uh . . .' He's hovering on these solid wooden boards. Even though the café's empty and we're mostly inconspicuous, I can feel the humid air is tense with his leg muscles working nervously beneath his skirt, beside me. And me, I'm flopped like a great pregnant lady. Doesn't he wonder how I can be so fat? Why is he still – is he really? Could he really be chatting me up? I never thought to have another man look my way.

'Uh . . . I need something not too intellectual to read on my nights off from here.'

I smile and take a deep breath and start to tell him about Angela Carter. He's never heard of her before and I tell him that he's got a treat in store.

It's mid-morning and the Greek yoghurt's not been delivered yet. So he says there's some home-made peach-and-honey ice cream I could have instead. Would that do? I say it sounds wonderful. He brings it and I can feel our baby give a pang at the sweetness.

I leave my things, my jacket, leopard-skin rucksack, Maugham, at the table (a risk, I know) and pop downstairs to the loo. He's in there, skirt hoisted around his hips in the pissoir in the cellar. He turns for a nonchalant smile.

'When's it due?' he asks as I take my place. He glances down at the hump of our child; I give his cock the once-over.

'Any day now,' I say.

'Do you want a boy or a girl?'

'I don't mind. Just so long as it's healthy and well.'

'Yeah, sure.' He nods approvingly.

*   *   *

Six mornings later he has to ring an ambulance for me and is there at the birth. My mother is due back from the continent the next day and she comes bearing all sorts of baby gifts. The baby has a fine leopard-skin fur. The waiter comes to my hospital bed with real lilies. Life's looking up. You sent your card and I'm writing this but I don't reckon I'll post it.